ALSO BY TOM MERRITT

United Moon Colonies

Lot Beta

Citadel 32: A Tale of the Aggregate

PILOT X

TOM MERRITT

PILOT X

INKSHARES

Published by Inkshares, Inc., San Francisco, California, as part of the Sword & Laser Collection
www.inkshares.com

Edited and designed by Girl Friday Productions
www.girlfridayproductions.com
Cover design by Dan Stiles

ISBN: 9781942645313
e-ISBN: 9781942645320
Library of Congress Control Number: 2016942384

First edition

Printed in the United States of America

To Ms. Lambert OBE

BOOK 1—AFTER

X

His flight was timeless. His ship, the *Verity*, was equipped with all manner of features to pass the time, entertain, research, educate, and more. He made use of none of them.

Mostly he wept. Not so much for what he'd done but for the need of doing of it. And for the fact of his survival. He could have let himself disappear with everything else. Often he wished he had.

But he hadn't. It was his punishment and his reward. He must live with the guilt, but more than that, he must live. It was his duty to tell the tale, help the others, and make certain it was not all in vain.

So he flew to the Fringe Cascade, a smaller civilization left mostly undisturbed by the disaster. If anyone knew best how to continue in the aftermath, it would be them, even if they didn't know why, which they likely wouldn't. Although fundamentally unchanged, they would still believe existence had always been like this. And yet they would be clever enough to know something had happened. When he explained what it was, they could help him deal with it.

A light went on at the console. A very important light. A light that usually demanded immediate attention. Pilot X looked at the light and laughed. He had been detected, and the light indicated the Fringe Cascade was still expecting him. They had scanned him and approved his approach, even though they should have no idea who he was anymore.

"We are approved for approach," Verity said.

Pilot X merely nodded. He hadn't spoken in parsecs.

The *Verity* lurched and threw him away from the console. His head jerked up to the transparent ceiling of the cockpit where Verity's voice came from. He imagined her scowling at him, though there was nothing up there but the curved window and the hidden speaker. Still, he knew she would be scowling if she had a face. She hadn't been pleased with his silence. He laughed again. That was two laughs since he had begun this trip.

Another series of lights went on. These did not make him laugh. These were bad. The *Verity* had been captured and was being pulled in. So he was expected but no longer welcome.

"Our approach is being restricted," Verity said. "They appear to be displeased."

Pilot X nodded again. Either they knew nothing or somehow they knew everything.

He'd find out why soon enough.

THE FRINGE

"Commander, I've got something."

"What is it, Specialist?" Commander Angtilik moved down the long row of seated scanners to Scanning Specialist 12's station.

"It's a match for a surveillance order. The *Verity*."

"The *Verity*? Don't know it. Who gave the order?"

The Specialist hesitated. "Uh, it says here you did, sir."

"What? When?"

"I don't know, sir. In fact I don't remember entering it myself. It just popped up like it's always been there."

"Nonsense. Maybe it's from upstairs. Damned odd to slap my name on it if it is. Don't worry, Specialist. Good work. Do try to pay more attention when you're authorizing orders, though. Could sound sloppy not to remember orders."

The Specialist looked doubtful. "Yes, sir. I've sent acknowledgment and provided approach for now."

"Good, good. What else do we have on it?"

The Specialist poked around on his interface for a minute.

"Not much, sir. The order only calls for an alert if the vessel is matched. It's called the *Verity*. No known origin. No known crew. One race. Alendan?"

"Alendan? Never heard of it."

"And that's it, other than—oh! My apologies, sir. It's a Level-One alert."

"What?! That's ridiculous." Level One was an all-hands emergency. The idea that a Level One could be spotted but nobody was expecting it or even remembered entering the order was one of the most disturbing things the Commander could think of.

"Well . . . capture it. I'll head upstairs and try to get to the bottom of this."

The Commander ran up to the Captain's office, but the Captain had already headed off to the Admiral's ready room. The Commander raced down the corridors to catch up and came barreling into the ready room, which was filled with top officers all staring at him.

"Ah, Angtilik." (It was spelled "Ngtyllik" and pronounced in a way not possible for most people with only one tongue, but "Angtilik" was how an Alendan would say it.) "I assume you can explain this?"

Crap.

"Somewhat, sir." This brought a perturbed look to the Admiral's face. The rest of the officers looked less than pleased. Nobody joked about a Level-One alert, and they all seemed to know even less than Angtilik did.

"Specialist Ramsey"—spelled "Rhmjsii"—"spotted the target just now on a ship called the *Verity*. Records show I gave the surveillance order at Level One signed off by you, Admiral. Neither the Specialist nor I recall the order, which is damned odd in this case. The ship's only details are a race of origin called Alendan. I'm not familiar."

A Captain from another part of the operation laughed. "You don't read fairy tales, then?"

"What's that supposed to mean, Fergranters?" the Admiral snapped. (Oddly enough, "Fergranters" was spelled "Fergranters.")

"Sorry, Admiral. The Alendans are characters from children's stories. A once-powerful race that could travel in time but reached too far and brought their entire people to destruction. Typical moral lessons and such—"

"And that's all we have?" the Admiral cut him off. Captain Fergranters was from the Cultural Relations arm. They could talk at length if allowed. "Please tell me this isn't some kind of joke, Angtilik—"

An aide interrupted the Admiral. "Admiral, we're getting a transmission from the ship."

"Is it already locked on approach?"

"Yes, sir. It's been captured on my orders," said the Commander.

"OK, so they can't pull much. At least we did that part right. Let's hear it."

A burst of static filled the room, followed by a perfectly normal-sounding voice speaking the dominant language of the Fringe Cascade.

"This is Pilot X of the *Verity* to the command of the Fringe Cascade. I mean you no harm. Doubtless your records about me are in disarray or even missing. I can clear up the confusion. Please allow me to land peacefully."

The message repeated.

"All right," said the Admiral. "Grant him his request. But make sure a well-armed battalion meets him to make sure it stays peaceful."

INSIDE THE FRINGE

Pilot X landed the *Verity* in a, dark, and mostly empty hangar. The usually bright silver-gray surface of his timeship seemed dull with the lack of anything interesting to reflect. He left the cockpit and stepped out of the tall cylinder that was the *Verity*. His ship was deceptively small, given its hidden singularity compartment, but still three times his height. He found himself face-to-face with a battalion of armed guards. An officer stepped forward.

"I am Commander Angtilik of the Fringe Cascade. Are you the one identifying as Pilot X?"

"I am."

"You've got a lot to explain, sir. And let me tell you, calling yourself an 'Alendan' did not go over well with the Admiral."

Pilot X sighed. "I can imagine not."

The guards took Pilot X into a gray room with soft padded walls. It had the sparse feel of many an interrogation room Pilot X had seen, although slightly more comfortable. He sat in a springy chair in front of a table made of high-quality material with the capability for displays and touch controls, though he saw no obvious way to activate them. Probably biolocked. Still, this felt more like an efficient meeting room than a prison.

He had left the *Verity* with nothing on him but his clothes, although one of his pockets was a back door into the *Verity*'s transdimensional chamber. He could reach his toolbox through the pocket, but he didn't have any plans to do so. The Fringe Cascade folks were militaristic but fair, in his experience. At least they had been. He hoped he hadn't changed that.

X

After a short period, the door opened and an older woman entered, wearing an understated uniform bristling with power and the tiny, almost nonexistent metal insignia of an Admiral of the Fringe Cascade.

"I'm Admiral Howtsendra. You may stay seated. You have cooperated well. You're obviously a man of honor and your ship is . . . well, your ship is beyond belief. So I'm conducting this interview myself. But you are observed and guarded should you be harboring any ill will toward me."

The Admiral walked to one side of the room and pressed part of the wall. A panel slid open, producing a second chair. She sat down and touched the table. It sprang to life.

"This"—she pointed to a block of text—"is an order that appeared in our system without explanation for a Level-One emergency response to a ship called the *Verity* carrying a pilot who is of the Alendan race. It is allegedly signed by me, though I never signed any such thing.

"This"—she pointed to another block of text with a waveform diagram and a small video—"is the transcript of our communication with you where you identified yourself as being from the ship the *Verity* and of the race Alendan.

"Pilot X, if that's actually your name, we do not find it humorous when someone breaches system security and forges the credentials of a flag officer. What do you have to say for yourself?"

"What do you think the Alendans are?" asked Pilot X.

"Dammit, I'm asking the questions, not you. You don't seem to have an accurate understanding of the trouble you're in."

"I can only answer your question accurately—or at least in a way you'll understand—if I know where to start. What do you think the Alendans are?"

"Humph." The Admiral folded her arms and stared at Pilot X for a long moment. "Captain Fergranters says they're a fairy tale about time-traveling aliens or some such. A moralistic tale about pride, I understand. I'm not familiar with it myself."

"Interesting." Pilot X rubbed his chin. "Well, Admiral, that is likely true now, but it is because of me. The fairy tale would be that the Alendans used their power for ill and destroyed themselves. Is that it?"

"Something like that," said the Admiral.

"It happened. I was the person who pushed the self-destruct button, so to speak. That's why I'm still here. Why I'm the only Alendan still here. The button was protected against the time change and I was close enough to press it, so close enough to be protected as well. As was my ship."

"Trash," the Admiral said and stood. "Why not work the Pineapple Planet into your story while you're at it! If you can't be serious, we'll lock you up until you feel more grave." She turned to leave.

"Well then, I intend to show you." Pilot X felt the power to create a paradox well up inside him. Nobody left could stop him. He felt the intention grow like a bubble and burst into inevitability. There was a knock on the door before the Admiral reached it.

She opened the door and a stunned guard stood outside next to Pilot X. "I'm sorry, Admiral. I don't know how he could possibly have got out. But he volunteered to come back." The Admiral nodded, unable to muster a coherent response as the second Pilot X stepped into the room and shut the door behind him.

"Verity says this is a rather stupid idea and we'd best not try it again," the second Pilot X said to the first. "I was right when I told me that earlier. But there's no stopping it now. Admiral, you'll need to instruct the guards to accompany me, that me"— he pointed at the sitting Pilot X—"back to my ship and let me inside. I'll only be in there a few seconds, I promise. Then I'll be right back here, as you can already see."

The first Pilot X got up and walked to the door. The second moved out of sight. The first opened the door and nodded toward the Admiral.

The Admiral hesitated and then said, "Um, escort Pilot X back to his ship and allow him to go inside. It's all right."

"Yes, Admiral," the guard said, and the first Pilot X left.

The Admiral turned. She accepted this. She wasn't gaping, but instead gave a stern, questioning look at the second Pilot X, who was now the only Pilot X in the room.

"Time travel," said Pilot X. "I am on my way to the *Verity* right now. I'll jump it back a few minutes. Enough for me to leave and walk over here just a moment ago, then the *Verity* will jump back to where she was right after she left. Your guards at the ship won't notice anything. I created a small paradox that apparently causes a tiny rip in time, according to my ship, and you now believe me."

"How do you know I believe you? Did you jump forward in time and ask me?" barked the Admiral.

"No, but I could have. Well, Verity would have been mad if I did. But no, I'm just guessing you're smart enough to figure this out."

The Admiral made a noise not unlike her earlier "humph" but more internalized and guttural. She sat down again and motioned for Pilot X to do the same. She touched a few more controls on the table and a recording system began. It flashed a discreet CLASSIFIED mark.

"Start talking," she said.

THE ELDERS

The Grand Chamber of the Elders of the Fringe was seldom used. The Elders preferred to conduct their business in the more comfortable and private chambers of their lodge. The secretive council that oversaw the Fringe Cascade rarely felt the need to intervene publicly in affairs, after all.

But on the rare times they were required to do so, they made use of the chamber to its full effect. The nine Elders would sit in a circle on a round silver-gray platform in the center of the chamber, surrounded by an audience. Each Elder sat in a simple but elegant silver-gray-fabric seat that faced inward toward the Elders across the circle. Nine screens were placed in a circle high above the Elders, and each showed the Elder opposite, allowing an audience member anywhere in the chamber to see some Elders directly and the rest on the screen.

A crowd of a hundred or so was usually allowed into the chamber, and the rest of the Fringe Cascade's inhabitants could watch the entire procedure remotely. It was theater, pure and simple.

At the moment, the chamber was empty, and Elder Angenhurt (spelled "Ngtenghirt") stood in the audience level, where she had been directing setup for the hurriedly required Discussions that were to take place. Elder Yoreshun ("Yorzexian") had just informed her of the full reasons why.

A lone pilot claimed to have flown out of the devastation of a Dimensional War. According to him, he alone survived. His race was supposedly one of the main combatants. He called them the Guardians of Alenda, who protected the secrets of dimensional physics. The pilot asserted he had no special knowledge of these physics himself, though his ship was capable of travel through them.

The Elders of the Fringe had no recollection of these races but had confirmed the high probability of such a war by studying the absences it left. For instance, an order to apprehend the pilot existed, but no one could recall creating the order or why. So the Elders of the Fringe decided to call the pilot before them before the Admiral and others learned more than was good for them.

"And that is all he told Admiral Howtsendra?" Elder Angenhurt asked.

"The only things of importance before we cut short the interview," Elder Yoreshun answered. "The Admiral showed unexpected initiative and curiosity in this regard. We believe it may be an effect of the Dimensional War that has thrown off our personality assessments, at least in regard to Pilot X."

"Then this will be a closed event?"

"Correct," answered Elder Yoreshun. "We'll use the chamber to show the public we conducted a thorough investigation. We have a seven-nines confidence that this will ease any provocative factors regarding his story."

Elder Angenhurt nodded and returned to preparing the chamber.

X

The seats remained empty and the screens dark. But the nine Elders of the Fringe sat in their ceremonial positions in their ceremonial starlight robes. Pilot X sat in the center of their circle. His black padded chair swiveled gracefully toward each Elder who addressed him. He worried it would make him dizzy, but they seemed to have perfected the technology.

There was no High Elder or Chief, but Elder Angenhurt seemed to have been nominated to begin the interview.

"Pilot X, claimed lone survivor of the race of Alendans, we bring you here to question you on your role in a Dimensional War that we determined must have taken place. Your ship and the evidence you gave Admiral Howtsendra imply you do not dispute this. We sit not in judgment of a crime, but in assessment of you entire. What you say here will not be the only determinative factor in assessing your standing with the Fringe. However, the more truth you describe, the more helpful it will be."

"I understand," Pilot X answered.

"We begin with a broad request: tell us everything."

"A broad request indeed, but I will try to address as intended. I will start with my beginning. Not my birth, but my beginning on the way to becoming who I am today."

"And who is that?" interrupted Elder Hough with a smirk.

"The lone survivor of the Dimensional War, the lone member of the Guardians of Alenda, and perpetrator of the Last Crime of Existence."

His statement was met with stunned silence.

"I became a Pilot when I successfully negotiated a return voyage to Alenda . . ."

BOOK 2—BEFORE

FIRST FLIGHT

"This is the *Valiant*, requesting permission for system entry."

"Roger, *Valiant*," system control responded. "Proceed to entry and submit credentials for orbit insertion point."

"Roger."

The tall dark-gray column of the timeship *Valiant* rotated from its orbital angle to a descent position and began to enter the atmosphere of the gray-green planet of Alenda below.

The *Valiant*'s trainee pilot, Apprentice X, turned to the Secretary.

The Secretary's smile didn't quite look complete. "Well done, Citizen X. You're almost there."

"Uh . . ." Apprentice X paused at the name change.

"He's Apprentice X," interjected the Instructor.

"Ah, my mistake," said the Secretary in a soft voice. "I meant no offense, *Apprentice* X."

Apprentice X tried not to grin. The Secretary was a legend for his leadership and diplomacy, but also legendary for his small gaffes. Apprentice X felt almost proud that he'd been the subject of one.

System control repeated their request for credentials, and Apprentice X turned his attention back to the flight test. He completed the rest of the procedures by the rules: entering coordinates, issuing ship-wide directives, guiding the *Valiant* from orbit into Capital airspace, and landing in the main shipyard.

"*Valiant* shows groundfall," he reported.

"Landing confirmed," system control responded. "Welcome to Alenda, Pilot X."

The small crew of officers that had been observing burst into applause. Even the Secretary clapped him on the back. "Get used to it, *Pilot* X. That's your name now."

Pilot X just grinned.

X

As they left the *Valiant*, Pilot X looked out at the fleet of smaller single-pilot ships parked nearby. Each one was a gray cylinder with rounded edges and a translucent cockpit area just slightly bulging out of the bottom. Older models were squat and the cockpit looked like a bump. The newer models were thinner and slightly taller, and the cockpit was almost flush with the rest of the surface. Each one could propel itself through time as well as traditional space. One of them would be his.

"Trying to decide which one you'll take?" asked the Instructor good-naturedly.

"I'll take any! They all look good to me," Pilot X laughed back.

"I think you should take that one." The Secretary pointed to one of the newer models that had a slightly silver sheen. "It's called the *Verity*. New stable onboard singularity with an expansive chamber and a top-notch AI."

"Are you serious?" Pilot X gaped. "I'll be time traveling straight out?"

"Very serious," answered the Secretary, shaking hands with the new Pilot. "Congratulations, Pilot X."

X

Alendans were the only true time travelers in the universe, and that ability was closely guarded. Only adults could be passengers on time-traveling vessels, and very few of those were qualified to pilot the ships. Pilot X felt truly honored to have that ability from the outset. And in a single-pilot ship! He could take passengers, but it was meant for solo voyages, meaning he would be sent on time-travel missions.

"You are destined for great things," the Secretary mused. "I can say no more. You'll find your first mission programmed aboard the *Verity* already. He—or she, your choice, I guess— will fill you in."

The Instructor shook Pilot X's hand and congratulated him again. The Secretary gave him the credentials he would need to show the guard and told him to take control of the *Verity* immediately, then he left.

The guard saw Pilot X's credentials were in order and waved him over to the *Verity* without ceremony. Still, this was the biggest moment of Pilot X's life. His first ship. His first command. His first job carrying the name he'd always hoped to earn. *Pilot.*

X

Alendans changed first names throughout their life based on their purpose, or what other societies would call an occupation. Pilot X had met an offworlder once who was thoroughly confused by it. Pilot X pointed out that the offworlders had multiple names at once. A first name, a surname, a nickname, a middle name, a religious name, a user name. So many names! *That* was confusing. At least the Alendans stuck to just two, and only one of those ever changed.

Each Alendan received a name at birth. That name had to be unique throughout Alendan history to avoid confusion. He was born the day single character names were finally allowed. So his name was X.

X

Until the age of twenty, each person's first name was their age from one to twenty. At age twenty-one, Alendans progressed to something like "Trainee" or "Student," or in X's case, "Apprentice." "Citizen" was what anyone without a purpose or someone between purposes was called. It was almost an insult. That's why it was odd to hear the Secretary use it earlier. Surely he was not confused that Pilot X had been an Apprentice? Still, it didn't matter now.

Every young Alendan anticipated the day they would receive their first real name. The name that made clear their purpose in society. They would carry more than one of these throughout their life, changing it as jobs and responsibilities changed, but the first name was always what one thought of oneself as truly being. He had wanted that to be Pilot X. And today that had come true. He would always think of himself that way.

THE ASSIGNMENT

The planet and the people of Alenda had borrowed their name from the city Alenda, which had it first. Of all the planets and moons that the Alendans inhabited, the planet Alenda was not the most densely populated, but you'd never know it in the city Alenda.

Skyscrapers not only went up but also sideways, even at heights near the edge of the atmosphere. A few buildings maintained hermetic seals and internal pressure so they could poke above the atmosphere and attain notoriety until the next building extended just past it.

But none surpassed the elegance of one of Alenda's smaller structures, the home of the Guardians of Alenda, rulers of the city, the planet, and the people of Alenda. It was five stories tall in the time Pilot X was visiting it. It had started as a simple mud hut and would eventually rise to seven stories.

It was home not only to the Guardians but also one location of their executive, the Secretary. Pilot X waited in the outer chamber of the Secretary's temporary Alendan reception room. It wasn't the Secretary's real office, but Pilot X wasn't high enough in stature to visit that office. Only the Guardians and certain Ambassadors in the Secretary's employ even knew where the real office was. Pilot X could travel in time, but he wasn't an officially recognized time traveler. He could only go where others directed him. Well, that wasn't strictly true. He could conceivably go wherever he wanted, but if he did so without permission, he would be dismissed and stripped of rank.

Which was why he fidgeted. The Secretary would only want to see him if he had done something wrong. He had only been piloting the *Verity* for a few subjective years. A normal career path would take him toward rising positions in the Alendan Fleet and eventual entry into the ranks of Supervisors or Instructors. Only at that point would he expect to be called to the Secretary's office—unless something very bad had happened.

A door opened. From behind its deep-brown wooden frame stepped the Secretary.

"Pilot X, so good of you to come. Right this way, please."

No one was that nice if they weren't about to drop a hammer on you, no one of the Secretary's rank, anyway. Pilot X braced himself.

The room was bare. Rich wooden shelves lined the walls, but nothing filled them. This wasn't the Secretary's main office, of course. Just a place for him to work while on Alenda in this time and location. Still, Pilot X found it odd that they had gone to the trouble of building in shelves without filling them with anything.

The Secretary motioned for Pilot X to sit in a red velvet chair. The Secretary took a stuffed brown leather chair for himself. There were only chairs in the room, no desk. Pilot X supposed the Secretary worked with his own data machine in his lap or something. There was a fireplace, however, and it was lighted and pleasant.

"Your commander has been telling me good things, X."

Pilot X remembered his training run when the Secretary had called him "Citizen." Now he dropped the first name altogether, something rarely even done by family. Pilot X stifled an internal giggle. Most said the Secretary acted eccentric because he moved through time so much. Pilot X kept in mind that he might in fact be meeting the Secretary *before* the Secretary had accompanied him on his qualification flight. After all, the Secretary would not let on to anyone—could not let on to anyone—in what order events were taking place for him.

"Thank you, Secretary," Pilot X responded.

The Secretary grinned as if they'd shared a joke.

"Good. I have an assignment for you, Pilot X." The Secretary paused as if unsure what he just said or what to say next. "It's a little beyond the normal portfolio of a Pilot." He stopped and eyed Pilot X. "But I know you're the one for the job."

The Secretary dropped an odd bundle on Pilot X's lap. Pilot X jumped. He hadn't even noticed the Secretary holding anything. A folded piece of stiff paper held a collection of other papers inside it. He picked it up gingerly.

"I expect you've never seen a folder before. Ancient stuff. Just brought it back from the Steel Times. It's all they use for record keeping there. So I played along. Sorry about that. You can scan the orders and read them normally or pretend to be an ancient and consume them as is. It's up to you. But all orders and details are contained in there, in any case. There are a few of those papers essential to the mission you'll need to keep, though, so don't get rid of the whole folder. You'll take the *Verity* out tomorrow. Then come back a few minutes from now, if you would. Do be careful on your way back not to run into yourself. Might be best to leave soon and give a wide berth to yourself. I'll meet you for a debriefing here in, say, twenty minutes?"

Pilot X's training kicked in and without thinking, he checked his doublechron and punched in the return time.

"Got it. I'll see you in twenty minutes." He smirked. He could share jokes too. Except he imagined they both got this one.

The Secretary laughed. "Your commander wasn't wrong. See you shortly, Pilot X."

The Secretary did not get up, so Pilot X showed himself out. He looked around carefully, half expecting to see himself, then headed out the back way from the administrative building.

In the *Verity*, he took a moment to look over the papers. Verity had wanted to scan and incinerate the orders immediately. It was the safest procedure, of course. These were literally State Papers. But he wanted the feel of the ancients. So he leaned back in his pilot's chair and shuffled through them as he suspected an ancient airplane pilot might have looked through a flight plan.

There wasn't much to go on. He was to proceed to a planet called Mersenne at a medium point in its development, hence the folder with paper. They had some light industry but no real space travel yet. At least nothing that could leave their own system. But they still used paper, so he'd have to hide most of his technology. He had instructions to land away from settlement and camouflage the *Verity*, then get some papers signed regarding an agreement with Alenda.

The assignment seemed too trivial for the Secretary to have taken time out of his busy schedule to deliver it personally. But it wasn't the kind of thing a time Pilot usually did, that was for sure. Two bundles of a dozen papers, each held together with a small metal object, were to be delivered to Mersenne's nominal leader, who went by the name Overseer Gaemmae. The Overseer was to review the copies and sign them both, then give one copy to Pilot X. Both copies were signed by the Secretary already.

The papers were confidential but Pilot X had clearance, so he looked them over. They were for something called a "technology binding." The Guardians of Alenda took responsibility for the development of dangerous technologies, especially time travel, throughout the universe. A technology binding was put into force when a civilization had developed or acquired something that could harm others beyond their own planet.

Mersenne seemed an unlikely candidate for this kind of arrangement. It was an agrarian society that hardly had any electronics. From what Pilot X could tell from the briefing, they hadn't developed anything that could destroy their own planet, much less harm anybody else's.

The binding documents themselves only identified "previous agreed-upon items." Pilot X supposed a separate document listed those items, but it was a document he didn't have. What he did know was that Overseer Gaemmae had agreed to the binding in principle but requested time to consult with his deputies before signing. The Secretary had agreed. Waiting periods were never a problem for time travelers. But rather than jump to the end of the waiting period himself, the Secretary had given the assignment to Pilot X. It was odd.

Even if the Secretary didn't feel Mersenne was worth his time, there were several Ambassadors that could have and should have taken the job. At the same time, Pilot X was excited. Although the Secretary often seemed mildly annoyed by Pilot X, he was never overtly hostile. People as powerful as the Secretary seemed annoyed by everyone. Maybe Pilot X was destined for greatness. The Secretary likely knew large parts of Pilot X's history, even the parts he hadn't experienced yet himself. Maybe he was only annoyed because he was impatient for this young Pilot X to become great.

Pilot X laughed at the thought. Ridiculous. How big of an ego did he need? This assignment was simple. Mersenne was a backwater. That was obvious. The Overseer was a time waster. The Secretary didn't want to spend any of his or his Ambassadors' valuable resources delivering papers to be signed. Pilot X was simply an errand boy. He finally allowed the *Verity* to scan the papers and prepare for departure.

X

Mersenne was beautiful. A lush green planet, half water, with golden seas in its north and south caused by some kind of ocean-dwelling microbe. Here and there some factory towns spewed smoke, but the planet had not progressed far enough to pollute itself. It was glorious.

Pilot X set the *Verity* down outside the capital city of Prime and put on his local clothing so he wouldn't stand out. He told the ship to blend into the trees around it, and set out to enjoy his walk into town. Prime was inhabited by about five hundred thousand people, but even so, it had a definitive end to the town, meaning he could set down in unfarmed countryside and walk toward the settlement as if it were a town of twenty. Once he passed into the buildings, the city spread out in a series of green plots where people lived, punctuated by small collections of businesses he learned were called villagelets. Prime tried to preserve the village way of life while gaining the advantages of a big city scale.

The village was like hundreds of others Pilot X had seen in training. Simple people going about their lives the best way they knew how. Nobody paid him any mind. His clothes and manner didn't stick out, so nobody noticed he only had two eyes. And they didn't seem to be concerned with strangers. There was no war here. No conflict. They benefited from the peace of the Guardians without even knowing it, for the most part. It made him smile.

After a long walk he reached the capital center and found the Overseer's offices. They weren't terribly impressive. A two-story brick building with a statue of something that looked like a winged horse outside. There were no guards, so very little ceremony. Signs pointed to the Overseer's office up a grand staircase, inside on the second floor. This was not a very hierarchical society, Pilot X guessed.

He finally reached his first familiar sign of bureaucracy in the form of an elderly woman wearing assistive devices on her three eyes seated outside the office of the Overseer. The people of Mersenne were like Alendans in most respects except for the number of eyes. Their ears were not as flat to the head either, but otherwise bipedal symmetry reigned.

All three eyes of the woman went wide as he approached. He wondered if his face looked mutilated or empty without the middle eye.

"You're not the Secretary, but you're Alendan!" she gasped. "Aren't you?"

"Yes. My name is Pilot X. The Secretary sent me to have the technology-binding papers signed. I've just arrived and came straight here. How do I go about making an appointment to see the Overseer?" Pilot X asked.

The woman laughed, dropping her shocked look at once. "Oh, you Alendans, so unnecessarily formal. Well, he's only with two people, after all!" She waved her hands at him in an odd gesture that Pilot X assumed was Mersenne for *don't worry*. "Go on in." She waved over her shoulder and got back to work.

Pilot X was not prepared at all for how informal Mersenne was. Only with two people? He felt like he was being tricked into making a protocol mistake, but he went toward the door. He could hear voices on the other side. Should he really open it? He turned to look at the lady, but she had forgotten all about him.

He turned the ancient knob and entered. What he saw made him reach for a weapon that he didn't have. His next thought was that it had been a mistake not to bring a weapon with him. A Progon drone and a Sensaurian SporePod were in the room with an elderly three-eyed man who must have been the Overseer.

"Well, well, so the Secretary couldn't make it after all. I thought you were time travelers! Ha-ha, come in, come in. I'm Overseer Gaemmae. This is Progon Representative 1367 and High Sensaurian Outreach Coordinator Thraw."

"Outrage!" droned the drone.

"We knew this would happen," gurgled the Sensaurian.

"I was not told they would be here," managed Pilot X. "What is the meaning of this?"

The Progon drone was a head taller than Pilot X. It was a thin metal shaft with four articulated limbs, two on each side, and treads for locomotion. Sensor pods ringed the top of the shaft in two rows and blinked occasionally.

Pilot X could hardly look at the Sensaurian. It was a green slug of a creature about half Pilot X's height contained in a yellow translucent life-support cylinder that made it look like the remains of something that had died. It smelled almost as bad.

"Now, now, this shouldn't come as a shock. If I'm about to sign an agreement to forgo the offerings of these two civilizations, you can't expect they won't try to talk me out of it, can you?" answered the Overseer. "Do you have the agreement?"

It took Pilot X a moment to realize the Overseer meant him. He tore his eyes away from the mortal enemies of the Alendans. He had never seen either species—if *species* was the right word for Progons—in real life.

He stuttered to life. "Y-yes, Overseer. Here." He handed the copies to the Overseer, who flipped through and then placed them on the desk.

"Now. I have heard all your arguments, and I understand. But the Alendans have proven themselves trustworthy and willing to benefit my people. I am sorry I can't give you what you want, honored representatives of the Progons and Sensaurians. I must sign."

"Outrage!" intoned the Progon again. Pilot X thought it odd for a machine to yell such an emotional response, but then the Progons were not machines at heart, only in body. He wondered if this was an actual Progon then, not just a mechanized drone. The thought of the incorporeal essence animating the machine gave him chills.

The drone continued. "I will return to my masters. We blame the Alendans, not you, Overseer. If you come to a realization, you know how to contact us. Do so quickly. We will take action, and we cannot guarantee this system's safety!"

So not an actual Progon. Just a drone. Before Pilot X could think more about what it had said, the Sensaurian responded.

"The Sensaurian Mind is one, as always. We must defend your system from the fraud of the Alendans and also"—the bulk of the sluglike beast shifted as if to indicate the Progon— "defend against Progon aggression, which the representative has made clear will not take your safety into account! We know you will do the right thing, Overseer, and you will see that we will as well. Take care."

The Sensaurian rolled out of the room, crushing Pilot X's toe in the process. The Progon made no pretense to hide its technology and disappeared. It looked like it transported itself out of the room, but Pilot X knew it was more likely just high-speed maneuvering, faster than Mersenne or Alendan eyes could see.

"My apologies, uh . . ." the Overseer stammered.

"Pilot X."

"Pilot? Interesting. My apologies, Pilot X." The Overseer signed the copies and picked one out to hand back. He held one hand up toward Pilot X's forehead.

The briefing had prepared Pilot X for this. He held his hand toward the Overseer's forehead, and they lightly rested their hands on each other's heads for a brief moment. Pilot X noticed the Overseer had two thumbs on his hand.

"It has been our duty and our privilege to serve you with such distinction," the Overseer then said, holding out one copy gripped formally at each top corner between his thumbs.

Pilot X recalled the proper response he had read in the briefing. Barely. "Your distinction is great, but the privilege and duty have been ours, pleasantly." Pilot X took the signed copy.

"Yeoman Alphaea will show you out, Pilot X. Thank you." The Overseer sat down and Pilot X turned to find a young man, probably about Pilot X's age, standing in the doorway.

"This way." The man smiled. Everyone on Mersenne was so cheery.

"It's not necessary, Yeoman," Pilot X said as they left the reception area. "I found my own way in, so I can find my own way back, I suppose."

"Not a problem. The Overseer was a little more concerned than he let on about your safety. I'll only accompany you to the city limits. I won't try to peek at your spaceship." He winked.

Pilot X liked the Yeoman.

As they walked, Pilot X asked the Yeoman about life on Mersenne. Was it as ideal as it looked?

"The woods were much bigger when I was young," the Yeoman said. "I know how important industry is for the betterment of all of us . . . but it makes me sad. I wish it didn't encroach on the beauty of nature. When we were young, we used to play in the forest. We'd pretend we were explorers on the Pineapple Planet."

"There are no pineapples there," Pilot X said without thinking.

The Yeoman laughed. "Ha-ha! Exactly. I'm glad you know the legend too. Those were such good times. But I can't take my boys there. Not to the Pineapple Planet, I mean, to the forest. It's been cut down for lumber and developed into housing. Mind you, I'm just sentimental. There are plenty of other woods. But when I was a boy, that's where we went to learn. Not some children's center."

"Children's center?" Pilot X asked.

"Oh yeah. That's the new consolidated schooling. It does work wonders. My boys are three times as smart as I'll ever be already. But I miss the old ways. Doesn't seem as fun. They seem to like it, though. Ah. Here we are. It was lovely making your acquaintance, Pilot X."

The Yeoman somewhat tentatively held his arm out toward Pilot X's forehead. Pilot X didn't hesitate but heartily thrust his arm out and grasped Yeoman Alphaea's head gently but firmly. This brought a smile to the Yeoman's face.

"Like a native," he said grinning. "Take care, Pilot X. Don't let them get you down." He looked up. "We're on your side."

Pilot X smiled at this and felt a bit better. He gave an Alendan salute as a last bit of punctuation, turned, and began the long walk back to the *Verity*.

On the way he wondered how dangerous it would be to leave the planet. You couldn't time-jump too close to a gravity well's center point. He should be able to time-jump as soon as he was out of the atmosphere, but that would be the trick. He understood the Secretary's motivations now. Having an unimportant Pilot show up meant Alenda's enemies would not act as aggressive. It meant less of a loss to Alenda should something go wrong, and a Pilot in a timeship had a better chance of getting away clean.

At least he hoped so. The *Verity* was still camouflaged, but he was a trained professional and found the place in the thin woods where he left her. Now that he was looking, he didn't think the camouflage was very good. From his point of view, the *Verity* looked like a big cylinder painted with leaves. She only blended in as well as a painted mural of autumn leaves would with real trees.

Verity sensed him coming and slid the entryway open. He walked in, and it closed behind him. It was as if he'd never been in the forest at all.

"I have launched a dozen signal replication probes in advance of our departure," Verity said. "Sensaurian ships are taking a defensive perimeter and ignoring them, but the Progons are actively chasing. Shall I launch another round?"

"You did what?" Was Verity provoking them?

"I monitored your conversation and several open ship channels from the Sensaurian and Progon fleets. The Sensaurians plan to intercept you as you leave. The Progons intend to shoot you down. I thought it wise to begin evasive maneuvers," she responded.

"Oh," Pilot X said. He'd been in combat on big Alendan ships with massive crews. The Alendans almost always outnumbered their opposition. He'd never contemplated being in battle alone. Assigned scouting missions with a fleet, sure, but entirely alone?

"Should we call for help?" he asked plaintively.

"I have sent an emergency alert to Alendan Central. However, response times may be as much as two Mersenne days."

"Two days?!" Pilot X yelled. "Why can't they just jump right to this point in time?"

"The response time includes factors of personnel avail-ability and prioritization of resources weighed against known time-stream risks and hostile-troop strength."

"In other words, I'm not important enough to risk jumping in and saving."

"You are not important enough to risk jumping in and sav-ing," Verity agreed.

"Ouch." Pilot X was stung by Verity's lack of hesitation.

"Under such conditions, protocol allows for latitude to preserve the assignment and personnel. The assignment is to return safely so the preservation conditions are easily merged."

Preservation conditions. Verity was trying to save his life. That made him feel a little better.

"Launch the second round of signal replicators," Pilot X finally said. "Is there a launch vector that—"

"The Sensaurians have left all starward paths open. It is likely they do not anticipate much preparation from you. The Progons have left only three viable departure vectors. Shall I choose the one with the lowest percentage chance of detection?"

"Yes," Pilot X said, trying to sound as if it had been a weighty decision. But then, whom was he trying to impress? Verity? His ship? Yes. He guessed he was.

"How many replicators have been launched and how many in operation?" he asked, showing a little initiative. Verity could report on how he handled this to any officer, he supposed.

"I have launched twenty-four. Ten remain in operation. Our departure vector options have dropped to two. One has a fifty-four percent chance of success. The other twelve percent. Shall we delay departure?"

"No!" he said. "But don't choose a departure vector." He had an idea.

"Go straight up, but launch twelve more signal replicators, this time replicating Progon, Mersenne, Sensaurian, and Alendan ships in equal measure."

"The chance of this stratagem succeeding is—"

"Just do it. And blast our signals in rotation," he cut her off. He didn't want to know.

"Verity on record protesting that forty-three percent chance departure vector was better plan. Verity conf—Departure vector options down to one at twelve percent. Verity on record supporting Pilot X decision for confrontational stratagem."

X

The Progons destroyed every signal replicator as soon as it left the atmosphere. The signal replicators could look to all sensors like any ship they had specs on. They were easily unmasked but caused enough confusion to buy time. Verity could mask her signals but not as effectively. She couldn't mask how much space she displaced. The gravitational effects were too fine in atmosphere. Pilot X's best bet was to pretend to be something else.

"Make sure at least three of the replicators—"

"Four signal replication probes have been sent on the previous high-probability successful departure vectors. Masking as meteor."

"Thanks, Verity."

"You're welcome," the ship said sweetly. Was it sweet? Could the ship sound sweet? He needed to focus.

"We have left atmosphere," Verity interrupted his thoughts.

This was the moment. Possibly his last moment. If he experienced another moment after this, it meant the plan had worked.

He experienced another moment.

Hanging before him was Alenda. Verity said, "Time jump initiated and complete. We are back at assignment return point. Beginning descent to twenty-five minutes after last departure. Apologies for the delay from assignment optimum of twenty minutes."

"Thanks, Verity. The Secretary can wait a few minutes," Pilot X grumbled. "I want an explanation."

But the Secretary wasn't there anyway.

"You just missed him," said a tall woman with dark skin. Her bearing was severe, but she looked at him with kind eyes. "He told me you'd be along and said I could take the contracts from you. He said you'd know what he meant." She smiled.

Pilot X almost pulled out the contracts, but he was angry. This was not a backwater assignment, and the Secretary had sent him into danger without preparation. He had almost died, and he didn't want to forgive that easily. If he argued with this person, he would lose his fire and end up handing over the contracts. So he chose not to fight. He didn't want to lose his anger, not just yet.

"That's all right," he said, grinning. "He'll know where to find me." Pilot X turned and left.

"Wait!" he heard the woman shout, but he didn't turn around. In fact he had the perverse idea that if he hurried, he could catch up with himself and stop him going at all. But he knew it would never work. Physics abhors a paradox. It took a lot more energy than a little anger to rip causality from its rails and change the course of a whole reality.

So instead he went to get a drink and a bite to eat. He felt his communication device buzz, so he turned it off. The only thing that bothered him was that the Secretary, being the Secretary, likely knew this is what he'd do. So why the charade?

X

Pilot X finished off his Alendaller sandwich. The fried beef patty within two thin but sturdy slices of Gorber bread was delicious. His only regret was that he hadn't ordered cheese. He looked at the small amount of beer left in his glass. He shouldn't have another. But he'd had enough of this one that he wanted another. But he needed to keep his head clear for when the Secretary found him. But his head would still be mostly clear after another. It was a third he needed to stay away from. But once he had another, he knew a third would sound like a grand idea.

The bartender started walking his way over to ask if he'd like another. The Secretary sat down next to Pilot X. The bartender did an about-face and left them alone.

"Assistant Le told me you didn't give her the contracts," the Secretary said without preamble. "Why didn't you give her the contracts?"

Pilot X looked the Secretary in the eye. The beer had kept the anger simmering. It began to boil again.

"My instructions were to return the contracts to you. I didn't know her. So I waited for you." Pilot X waved dramatically. "And here you are?"

"Are you drunk?" the Secretary asked, laughing.

"No," Pilot X said firmly. He was not. At least he was pretty sure he wasn't. Not on one beer. He couldn't be.

"So you didn't give Assistant Le the contracts because you were sure I'd chase you down in a bar?" the Secretary said.

Pilot X wagged his finger. He knew intellectually that was not an appropriate way to address the Secretary. Was he drunk? He put his finger down. No. He wasn't. "No," he said simply. "I did not know Assistant Le was called Assistant Le. I did not know she worked for you. You said you would meet me for a debriefing. You weren't there. The contracts were obtained under combat conditions, and I felt strict adherence was called for in following your orders." He felt like somehow he had rambled, but it all made sense to him. It was all true. And it all needed to be said. How long had he been talking?

"So you were afraid Assistant Le was a Progon spy?"

"I made no such assessment," Pilot X said. "It was not mine to make in either direction."

The Secretary sat back at this, looking impressed. "It's a fair point. If you were lately of combat, you shouldn't give critical mission documents to anyone without requiring a determination of identity. I'm impressed, X. You studied your regs, it seems. At least if there was truly combat. But come now. What kind of combat would you see on Mersenne? Some rifles aimed at you? Did a bandit on a horse mug you? What?" The Secretary chuckled.

There it was again. This time it wasn't funny. "I am *Pilot* X, Secretary. And the *Verity* has filed my flight report. We came under direct attack by Progons and defensive threat by Sensaurians when leaving Mersenne. Their representatives threatened me directly in the Overseer's chambers." Pilot X tried not to look smug, but he expected he looked smug.

"Well. *Pilot.*" The Secretary left the *X* off this time. "That is another matter indeed. There was no intelligence that either race would be there. I will review your report. The documents?"

The Secretary was implying he was surprised, but he wasn't acting at all surprised. And he shouldn't be. He was the Secretary. *Not* knowing about Progon or Sensaurian presence at any important point in space-time would be gross incompetence or worse.

Pilot X handed over the papers.

"Thank you, Pilot. X. We'll be talking soon." The Secretary turned and left.

The bartender finally sauntered over, looking sympathetic. "Boss?" he asked.

"Yeah," said Pilot X.

"Another?" asked the bartender.

"Yeah."

THE RECOMMENDATION

Puffy pink clouds drifted through the Alendan skies, hinting at coming rain, but the day was otherwise excellent as Pilot X met Ambassador Uy in the shipyard. Ambassador Uy was one of his favorite diplomats. Pilot X often received assignments from the Ambassadorial staff, though usually not in person.

"You've been an excellent Pilot," Ambassador Uy said as they stood outside the *Verity*. "I have to say, more than just a Pilot. Your understanding of the tripartite peace ranges far beyond what I would expect from someone driving a timeship. No offense intended."

Unlike many diplomats, Ambassador Uy seemed to mean what he said.

"Well, I've had some experience with the Sensaurians and the Progons directly. It helps." Pilot X hadn't had any more direct assignments from the Secretary since his blowup in the bar, but his assignments seemed to always put him somewhere near a Progon mech ship or a Sensaurian pod flight. He had wanted to apologize for his attitude but then never got the chance.

"You certainly have. I've never heard of anyone but the Secretary being in a room with a Progon and Sensaurian representative at the same time!"

Pilot X laughed. "Yeah. Not an actual Progon, I don't think, but I could never be entirely sure. That's a civilization that is utterly alien. I don't know if it's even proper to call them a people. But they are a civilization."

Pilot X admired the precision of the Progon way of doing things. His dealings with them had become entirely predictable. Despite their occasional off-key emotional outbursts, which he suspected were a poor attempt to speak his own language, the Progons had a cool logic to how they conducted themselves. They needed to be stopped, of course, but in the way a falling rock needs to be stopped. At least that was Pilot X's opinion.

"Listen, I'd like to ask a favor," Ambassador Uy said, becoming serious. "I'd like to recommend you for a diplomatic post. I get a say in the Ambassadors that train under me, and I think you'd be stellar. An excellent outsider perspective with real-world experience. I hope you don't mind, but I surveyed your public records and you certainly meet the qualifications."

Pilot X was stunned. "But I've never studied!" he protested.

Ambassador Uy shook his head, smiling. "Neither have half the Ambassadorial Corps. The students who study diplomacy are often at a disadvantage in real fieldwork. They're excellent on theory but have a hard time translating it into practice. That's why we have a mix. It's why I prefer the three-person team that I keep. Ambassador Tri is an excellent academy-trained Ambassador, but my other trainee, Ambassador Ku, is leaving. Ambassador Ku had excellent field skills. I think you would too. Will you consider it?"

Pilot X wasn't sure.

"Don't answer yet. I'll send you some reasons why I think it would be good for you and for me, and for the Guardians of Alenda in general. Look it over. If you're still not convinced, I'll understand. But just look it over. Will you do that?"

Pilot X smiled and nodded.

Ambassador Uy was sincerely pleased. "Excellent. We'll talk soon."

"We can talk in five minutes if I come back to right here," Pilot X joked. "But that might throw off your prepared remarks. Maybe I better stick to continuity this time."

Ambassador Uy laughed at this somewhat off-color joke for a timeship Pilot. They were forbidden from messing with the timeline on their own initiative. The joke could have been taken in poor taste. It wasn't. Ambassador Uy wished him well and left.

THE MISTAKE

Pilot X hung over the Moon of Pantoon, waiting for his passenger, Economist Rex, to return by pod shuttle from the surface. Pantoon was a universal trading post but allowed no non-Pantoonian vessels on its surface. All visitors traveled to and from the surface in a local invention called pods. They looked like huge glowing plastic balls. You got the impression they were translucent when you saw them from the outside, but that was just a quirk of their manufacture. What seemed to be the outline of a passenger was some kind of surface-conduit system that managed the propellant of the pods.

Pantoon's orbital space was alive with floating sparks as pods lifted off and descended, ferrying trade representatives from hundreds of civilizations back and forth. It was a glorious traffic nightmare. Pilot X still didn't understand how the little things got off the surface. Admittedly, it was a small world, so the escape velocity wasn't high, but the pods had no rockets. They weren't flung into the air or ferried up by another launch vehicle. They just fired up their engines and flew up until they left the gravity well, arcing gracefully toward their destination.

It seemed impossible but there they were, hundreds of them, currently defying the laws of physics.

Pilot X had never been to the surface of Pantoon, but he'd studied up on the pods. If he was more conspiratorially minded, he might have disbelieved the reports, but there were too many of them from too many varied sources for it to be a hoax. It was a trade secret so closely guarded that most Pantoonians were not instructed in how it worked. The technology was never shared and pods were never exported. Like the wide-bodied canal boats of Gerice on Alenda, this was a mode of transportation unique to one spot.

While he waited, Pilot X looked over the information Ambassador Uy had sent. It was compelling. Pilot X would continue to pilot the *Verity*, which would be assigned to Ambassador Uy's diplomatic service. Pilot X might have to occasionally act as a Pilot for other Ambassadors, but always as a courtesy and not frequently.

He would get a huge advancement in rank and privilege and learn even more about the workings of the tripartite peace that kept most of time and space stable. He wanted to know more too. Ever since his run-in with the Progons and Sensaurians, he suspected there was more going on between the three civilizations than anyone let on.

He knew Mersenne was not particularly resource rich. It was not particularly strategic either, or at least he didn't think so. It was extremely odd that both Progons and Sensaurians risked violating the peace to prevent the agreement he had carried. He wanted to know why. And he wanted to know why the Secretary had chosen him to carry it. It was so far back in the timeline that it must be important. He'd been hoping to visit Mersenne later in its history, but he hadn't had the chance. Mersenne was not an approved recreational destination. In fact, from the little public information he could find, the planet had a sad, short history, relatively speaking. No civilization lasted throughout time and space except the Progons, Alendans, and Sensaurians. And even those three didn't last all the way to the end, apparently. Only one civilization knew the real fate of the universe. The Fringe Cascade guarded the end points in time and space, marking a border that couldn't be crossed by any civilization.

That's why time travel was so heavily guarded. It's why the Alendans felt such weight and responsibility. It's why they had come into cold conflict with the only other civilizations that had a semblance of time travel. And, less important in the grand scheme, it's why he couldn't just up and visit Mersenne. Becoming an Ambassador might give him a chance to return. He'd love to check in on Yeoman Alphaea and see if he rose to success. He hoped he did.

Verity interrupted his thoughts. "Economist Rex's pod has begun its ascent."

"Thanks, Verity. Plot-jump to his last departure point. Then file a plan to visit Ambassador Uy."

"At what time point would you like to visit Ambassador Uy?"

Pilot X hadn't thought about this. No need to keep the Ambassador waiting. "Let's say one day after he submitted these reports to me."

"Plans filed."

Pilot X noticed one of the distant pods connecting with one of the other ships began to shake. That was odd. The dockings were usually so elegant. He noticed a few more rough dockings happening here and there. Maybe something was up with the pod navigation system. Was it centralized? Nobody but the Pantoonians knew, but that could explain a problem affecting multiple pods at once. It was an interesting insight into pod engineering.

Some of the other pods seemed to be shaky in their ascents as well. He checked Economist Rex's pod, but it seemed to be gliding up normally. Then out of the corner of his eye, he saw an explosion on another ship. Explosions in space were sometimes easy to underestimate. There was not a lot of fire and no shock wave. But that just made it more startling.

A Trellian cruiser had flashed a bright light and swung orthogonally out of its orbit, jolted by something. It almost looked like it had been hit by a missile, but there were no hostile ships out here. It didn't look like an internal problem, but it must be.

"Verity, what caused that Trellian ship—"

"The Trellian cruiser was hit by a pod at high speed. The pod did not properly slow its ascent."

Well now, that was damned odd. Something must be wrong with the pod-guidance system. He checked again on Economist Rex, but still saw nothing unusual.

Verity spoke up. "I have filed an observation report with Pantoon control, but there was no response other than to acknowledge receipt. No alerts have been issued. No hostiles have been detected."

By this point, Economist Rex's pod was within docking range and was gliding slowly in to connect with the *Verity*.

Alendan timeships were built so you could open the small cabin in a vacuum and not lose any air, at least not much to speak of. What little that might leak around the force shields was easily replaced by the gargantuan quantity the ships could access from their amazing singularity chambers. It was one of the ships' great efficiencies. No air scrubbing and circulation equipment was needed when you had a small planet's worth of room available that didn't add any weight to the ship.

The singularity chambers were a stable wormhole that led into what was essentially a pocket universe, though infinitesimally small when compared to a normal universe. Storage, passengers, supplies, and agriculture—all fit on board. Not technically on board, of course, but easily accessible. And since it wasn't technically on board, the timeship didn't have to provide thrust for it. The trick was to move the wormhole's open end as the ship moved through space-time. But Alendan science had figured that out, which meant there was always enough air to make docking trivial.

The *Verity* slid open the door to the main cabin as soon as Economist Rex's pod pushed up tight against it. The only concern was not to depressurize the pod, so the cabin's force shield was extended around it, holding the pod to the *Verity*.

Once the shield was secure, Verity signaled the pod that it was safe to open. The pod did a check of its own, and when satisfied, began the process of loosening its circular porthole. It was a loud and slow process, but eventually the many layers of shielding unlocked like a puzzle, and Pilot X could see Economist Rex standing inside, waiting to come out.

"Welcome back, Economist Rex."

"Fly!" yelled the Economist, and then fell to the ground in a heap. Standing behind him was a Sensaurian in body armor.

"We meet again, Pilot X," said the Sensaurian. "I've been looking so forward to seeing you."

How did it know him? Was this the same Sensaurian he had seen on Mersenne? That Sensaurian diplomat had been in a yellow bucket. This one was a green sluglike being, as were all Sensaurians, but Pilot X was not familiar enough with Sensaurians to tell if it was actually the same one. It had squeezed itself into a suit of translucent plasteel equipped with eight different extensions for manipulating the outside world. The Sensaurian itself was locked into the middle and controlled the limbs from there. It was like looking at an octopus standing up on its side.

"You don't remember this aspect of us, of course. But we remember everything."

Pilot X realized it didn't really matter if he had met this Sensaurian before. They were a hive consciousness and could send parts of their consciousness backward in time. So all Sensaurians would potentially remember meeting him on Mersenne, and this one might even have knowledge of his future.

"Well, I don't recall you, in fact. But what do you want? What have you done to Economist Rex?" He knelt down to look at him; he was alive but breathing heavily.

"We have only stunned him. We wouldn't want a diplomatic incident. Wouldn't want a *war*, would we?" The Sensaurian gurgled and made slurping noises that Pilot X assumed might be meant as laughter.

"Well, I think you may have messed up there. Pantoon won't take kindly to you commandeering their pods and abusing their visitors."

"Oh, but they won't mind. As of today, Pantoon has agreed to join the Sensaurian Civilization. A great day for Pantoon and all Sensaurians. Some parts of us have been assigned to greet representatives from every civilization to welcome you to the new Pantoon. We mean no harm and will continue trading activities here without interruption."

Pilot X could not tell if the Sensaurian smiled. He couldn't tell if the Sensaurian had a face. But it certainly sounded from the voice coming out of the translucent suit's speakers like it was happy.

"The Trellians seem to have come to harm," Pilot X pointed out.

"An unfortunate accident," the Sensaurian purred. "There was some misunderstanding of these pod controls. It seems a few rebels wanted to withhold information about how they worked. They have been dealt with."

A chime from the *Verity* indicated a system-wide announcement was incoming. Pilot X told Verity to put it on speakers.

"Attention, ships in orbit. This is the Pantoonian Executive. As most of you know by now, we have . . . agreed . . . to an affiliation with the Sensaurian Civilization. The Sensaurians have promised not to change our operations in any way but will install a permanent presence on the planet and of course receive access to our archives."

Pilot X let out a low whistle. Pantoonian archives held all the secrets of Pantoon, including how the pods worked. This essentially ended Pantoon neutrality and would shake the universal economy to its core.

The Executive continued. "We apologize that interference by rogue elements has caused some damage by pods. The situation has been rectified and will not be repeated. Sensaurian representatives have reached out to each of you to sign an acknowledgment of the new situation. We understand that not all of you have the authority to act on behalf of your own civilizations. This is merely an acknowledgment of the situation, promising you will inform your superiors, nothing more."

The Executive signed off.

A coup. That's what it is, thought Pilot X. They would get every civilization—almost every one was represented here— to sign acknowledgment. It didn't need to be binding; it just needed to be known. Then no one could claim ignorance and any move against Pantoon, even economically, could be treated as a provocation.

"I'm afraid your Economist Rex tried to struggle with me as I boarded our pod. You'll have to sign the acknowledgment, Ambassador X."

"I'm not an Ambassador, I'm a Pilot," X responded automatically.

"Oh, my mistake, I guess. I do so forget when I am sometimes. Pilot X. Could you please acknowledge the situation and inform the Guardians of Alenda of its existence?"

This Sensaurian knew him. Maybe knew the future him. It seemed to think he would become an Ambassador. But how could he? If he became the Alendan who acknowledged Sensaurian superiority over Pantoon, it would ruin his diplomatic career before it ever began. It wouldn't matter that it was bad luck.

He had to find a way out of this. No, he *would* find a way out of this; otherwise, the Sensaurian would not have mistakenly called him Ambassador. He realized this is what his teachers had warned of as a "confidence paradox," which came with all manners of horrible possible side effects. He distracted himself with the facts of the situation.

Economist Rex lay on the floor inside the *Verity*, unconscious but otherwise safe. The Sensaurian stood in the pod at the entryway, but hadn't actually entered the *Verity* yet.

That was it.

"Verity, close the door."

The Sensaurian made a noise that was cut off by the door sliding into place.

"Verity, find a point in Progon space-time that is diplomatically safe for Alenda but where tensions between Progon and Sensaurians are at a high point."

"There are five points that have above ninety percent hostile Progon-Sensaurian tension and above seventy percent Alendan diplomatic safety rating," responded Verity.

"Pick the one with the highest safety for me and jump," Pilot X answered.

The ship gave a minor shudder, an effect of the attached pod being carried along with them. Verity had not released it.

"Verity, open the door."

The capsule door slid open. The Sensaurian still stood there.

"Where are we?" it asked.

"Progon space," answered Pilot X. "When are we, Verity?"

"At the height of the Fruitless Expansion War, known by Sensaurians as the War of Attrition, or in their language—"

"It gets the idea," Pilot X interrupted.

The Sensaurian was quiet.

Pilot X waited.

"What do you intend to do?" the Sensaurian said, its voice a challenge.

"I intend to withdraw my force field from around your pod and leave you in Progon space during one of your most bitter wars, and let the Progons do with you what they will."

"It does not matter," the Sensaurian said. "This segment is but an infinitesimal part of us. It matters not if it dies."

"But it won't die right away," Pilot X explained. "It will be captured and examined. The Progons of this time will know everything it knows. Granted, they can message through time, but 'this segment' contains rich information they couldn't glean otherwise. They also get a Pantoonian pod to examine. Big tech advantage. Go ahead and think about that along with the rest of your hive mind. I know you contacted them already. I'll give you a moment."

The Sensaurian remained motionless for several moments.

"I prefer you not do that. What do you want?"

"Convince me not to," Pilot X said.

"How?" asked the Sensaurian.

"Start by leaving Pantoon alone."

"We do not know much about Pantoon. We cannot promise that."

"Yes, you can. *You* can remember. This segment will remember. And I can take it back."

"The Pantoonians will notice your absence. They will be angry you took the pod here and risked discovery."

"I'll return us to the second we left. They won't notice a thing unless you tell them."

The Sensaurian paused.

"We cannot leave Pantoon. It would be a disgrace. We know this. We risked much taking the moon; it would be too devastating."

"More devastating than the Progons recovering modern information from you directly?"

"Progons capture pieces of us regularly. They do not learn much."

The Sensaurian's resolve was stiffening. Probably as it integrated better with the Sensaurians of this time.

"Sure. That's true," said Pilot X. "But they're usually from the same time period. When segments have been sent back from the future, their future knowledge is carefully guarded. Yours isn't. You weren't prepared for this. The Progons of this age will make great use of this. Verity, prepare to withdraw the shield and eject the Sensaurian. The vacuum should keep his information well preserved."

"Shutting down force field now."

Well done, thought Pilot X. Withdrawing the field from the pod was instantaneous. Verity was bluffing.

"Wait," said the Sensaurian. "We are not unwilling to negotiate. But you exaggerate. Time cannot be changed. What happened in this war has already happened."

"Has it?" Pilot X knew this was largely true. "Timelines exist in bundles. Certain points are fixed because the bundles always converge there. And in a sense you're right, because all the bundles exist in a sense. But are you willing to jump to a new bundle? A bundle where the Progon war ends up the same but rages farther and higher and strengthens them more? Sometimes cataclysmic events can wipe out whole timelines and replace them. Are you willing to risk that this isn't the beginning of one?" Pilot X knew he was oversimplifying, but he was trying to strike the tone of a Guardian of Alenda who knew the intricacies of timelines. For he was Alendan. Everything he said was broadly true, although he exaggerated how common it was. Switching across bundles was difficult. Rewriting whole timelines was almost impossible. Almost.

"We need not be exclusive," said the Sensaurian.

What was this? A bargaining point? Now Pilot X was out of his depth. He'd hoped he could intimidate the Sensaurian into just backing down.

"What do you mean? I don't want to date you." The Sensaurian didn't get the joke.

"That is not the proposal. We do not have to be the only ones with a presence on Pantoon. We do not have to be the only civilization with access to Pantoonian archives. The Alendans could do so as well."

Pilot X knew little of negotiating, but he sensed he shouldn't give in too fast. Plus, he would need to convince the Pantoonians to go along with moving from total independence to having two overlords. Wait. Not overlords. Embassies. And to head off Progon trouble, why not give them one too? But how to convince the Pantoonians? Just the reduction in Sensaurian influence alone might be enough, but—

"The archives," he snapped, causing the Sensaurian to jerk. Then Pilot X remembered something. If he proposed his plan to this Sensaurian segment, the entire Sensaurian Civilization would remember it and have time to plan a countermove. Had they already?

"Verity, take us back as close as you can to our departure from Pantoon. I don't want more than an eyeblink."

"Moving," said Verity, as he felt the timeship jostle against the extra weight from the pod.

The Sensaurian was motionless, communing with the current Sensaurian state. It took less time than before, likely because they had centuries to prepare. Were they prepared for him before? Maybe they hadn't fully integrated. Maybe it was a trap. He would find out soon enough.

Before the Sensaurian could speak, Pilot X said, "You must not take access to the archives. You must offer the same affiliation and presence to the Progons." He paused and then added, "And you must not remember the conversation we had in the past."

He expected resistance especially to this last point. It was a wild hair.

"We do not remember this conversation. We agree to your terms."

The Sensaurian was probably lying, but Pilot X had the agreement he wanted. He couldn't prevent traps now, in any case. He had no idea what form they would take.

"You will contact the Alendan Ambassadors, the Progons, and the Pantoonians. Once that's done and confirmed, I will release your pod. Verity, close the door and secure the pod."

The door closed. If all went well, which Pilot X fully expected it wouldn't, the Pantoonians would protect their secrets and benefit from closer trade ties and a permanent tripartite presence. And who knew? The interaction of the three civilizations might calm things down overall.

X

Pilot X left Economist Rex's hospital room. The Economist was recovering well and would be back on his feet soon. He thanked Pilot X profusely, which embarrassed the Pilot a little. He had just left the Economist lying unconscious in front of the pod for most of the time.

Only after the rather stunned Ambassador Uy had contacted Pilot X to confirm what was being proposed did Verity open its door again. And only after an official Alendan Ambassadorial team and a Progon envoy arrived and were confirmed safely on Pantoon did Pilot X release the pod. And only after all that was done had he tended to Economist Rex. Still, he supposed the Economist had missed all that, and in his mind, Pilot X had probably got rid of the Sensaurian and raced him back to Alenda and safety. The Economist had not yet been brought up to speed on events, and the doctor had warned Pilot X not to bring it up quite yet.

As Pilot X neared the front doors of the hospital, a Messenger arrived. How genteel. Was it a birthday party? Some kind of anniversary soiree? Physical Messengers were usually only sent as some kind of highly stylized method of inviting someone to a personal event. It was the highest of fashion in Pilot X's home space-time.

"Instructor X?" the Messenger asked, approaching him. This stunned him. He had never been an Instructor, nor did he have plans to be. He was hoping Ambassador Uy's plans would make him an Ambassador, not an Instructor.

"*Pilot* X, if that's who you're after," Pilot X answered.

"Oh!" The Messenger looked very surprised. "My apologies, I've come to the wrong place," he said and turned on his heels and left.

Well, well. So Pilot X would someday be Instructor X and someone would send a Messenger to him and get the date wrong. Oops! Spoiler! He wished he would have played it cool now and found out a little more info. Well, he supposed he'd have to wait a few years. One couldn't become an Instructor unless you exited a main corps—like the Diplomatic Corps, for instance. And he was only just now on his way to Ambassador Uy's to get that possibility off and running.

X

Ambassador Uy's office was in an unfashionable corner of the diplomatic complex. A curtain with a broken loop hung askew across the window. Dust coated random surfaces, puffing and moving on its own due to a crack in the window glass. Piles of data-storage devices from several eras cluttered the shelves alongside ancient paper books stored on their sides and a few clay masks from foreign planets. The desk was old and wooden and creaked whenever anyone touched it. The Ambassador didn't even have the excuse of it being temporary. His team was assigned to Alenda.

The office did not inspire confidence. Pilot X assumed he wouldn't be offered a better one, and thought he might turn down an office and just work out of the *Verity*. The fact that he could continue to pilot was a great asset to Ambassador Uy, given the amount of travel his team did. That was one of the reasons Ambassador Uy had recruited Pilot X. He'd have to serve as Ambassador Uy's trainee for a couple years and pilot some other Ambassadors around, but that was all right. He couldn't expect to get his own field post right out of the gate.

Ambassador Uy leaned back and chuckled. "Pilot X. How'd you like to have your own field post right out of the gate?"

Pilot X choked.

"Don't look so surprised. You're the brave Pilot that stopped the Sensaurians from occupying Pantoon without firing a shot. You don't *know* how hot to hire you several future-posted

Alendan Ambassadors were. But our rules are very specific about using time-sensitive knowledge for persuasion. I lucked out. I never got posted in a place where anyone had heard about what you did and I recruited you anyway. In fact, I got accused of cheating by more than a few fellow diplomats, but they're just jealous. I wanted you for fieldwork, and now there's no reason to wait. You're preapproved, son!"

Pilot X choked some more.

"What do you say, Ambassador X?"

"Yes," Ambassador X croaked.

THE CORE

He spent his first few weeks as an Ambassador attending many meetings and parties. Ambassador X's kind of meteoric rise could cause jealousy, but he didn't feel it. Everyone seemed genuinely enthusiastic about what he did on Pantoon.

"You've set the table for peace! An actual peace between the three parties," said one aged Ambassador who must have traveled enough to know whether what he was saying was true. "I don't mean some glorified truce like we have scattered all through the timeline. I mean locking down threads and reducing war to a minimum. A star-burning *peace*, I say!" He slapped Ambassador X on the back and took a drink, his eyes glittering with the brandy.

X

His initial missions were mostly local and somewhat ceremonial. He went to Layglifer, the nearest planet to Alenda, to confirm the yearly alliance and friendship of the two planets. He sat at a table for a short period of time with an Ambassador from Layglifer, signed an actual piece of paper with an actual pen, and then went to an amazing dinner.

He flew the Chief Guardian of Alenda to Pantoon. The Chief Guardian was a ceremonial post. He would meet with the High Sensaurian and the Progon Central Commune Unit. In other words, the highest-ranking but least powerful officers in each civilization were getting together.

Ambassador X also did some low-level trade negotiations between various small civilizations here and there. He even settled a transit path dispute with the Fringe Cascade using his experience as a Pilot.

Nothing he did was historic. Nothing he did made a real difference. After a while the novelty of ceremony wore off. He kept his complaints to himself and tried his best to enjoy the high life he now lived. He felt guilty for not being more excited. Many people would eagerly trade places with him. No one on Alenda was actually impoverished, but others in the universe were. Still, he wasn't ungrateful, just bored. That wasn't his fault, was it?

Assignments like this went on for years until one day, Ambassador Uy called him in for what he assumed was a normal check-in. Ambassador Uy had aged. His face looked lined and his hair was gray. At least this time. Alendans didn't always meet each other in chronological order, but Ambassador Uy tried to. He was old-fashioned that way.

"Ambassador X," he smiled and stood in greeting. His smile as always was genuine and warm. "Sit down. This isn't the last time we'll meet for you, but it is for me. I'm sorry not to make a synchronous end to our relationship, but I think you'll understand. Well," he chuckled, "I know you will. I just came from your last meeting with me. Risking a paradox there, I suppose." He chuckled again. "Ambassador X, I'm putting you up to the Secretary to replace me. I know you've been underused, and I apologize for that. It's the nature of our business sometimes. It may have felt boring, but it was a great service to me. It could have been seen as an insult to send a staff Ambassador for some of the ceremonial duties you've taken on. Your celebrity helped there. Some of the smaller logistical matters you've handled so well would have been blown out of proportion if I'd taken them. Your newness helped there. But you've served without complaint, and for that I thank you."

Ambassador X nodded.

"There is one more assignment I must ask you to take before I can step down, because it would not be appropriate for you to do it after you took my place."

"Of course, Ambassador. What is it?"

"I need you to attend a meeting with the Alendan Core."

Ambassador X's pulse rose. The Alendan Core was the oldest continuous linear society on Alenda. It predated the ability to travel through time. Time-traveling Alendans had confirmed its existence back into preindustrial times, though it had been called different names in its history. Its members forswore time travel in order to maintain a unique linear perspective on society, which they offered for the benefit of whoever might want it.

Their activities were shrouded in mystery.

"I would be honored," said Ambassador X.

"We'll see about that," answered Ambassador Uy.

It was a childhood dream of every adventurous Alendan to be approached by the Core. Ambassador X couldn't understand Ambassador Uy's response, but he wasn't given more time to think about it.

"Every quarter the Diplomatic Department sends a representative to meet and speak with the Core. Since the Core doesn't travel through time, they request we not provide any information except strictly what they request. They don't

expect us to keep track of where in time they are in relationship to where we've been, so they tailor their questions very
narrowly. Sometimes they don't even ask anything but merely
meet to assure us they still exist. Sometimes they don't even do
that. But we send someone every time anyway."

"Who will I meet with?" asked Ambassador X.

"I don't know. We never know," he said and grunted dis-
missively. "We keep the agreement. We take notes. We report
back. The report gets logged by the Ambassadorial Division
of Chronography, and we move on. I don't even know why we
do it, really. They never give us any information. But still they
provide a valuable service in other ways, historical mostly, so
it's best to keep them happy, I suppose."

"When and where?" Ambassador X asked. Ambassador
Uy's attitude was dampening his spirits just a little.

"A couple years ago." Ambassador Uy looked down.
"Before your encounter on Pantoon. We, uh, actually forgot to
meet with them, to be honest. We always try to schedule the
appointments before they happen, but they understand when
we don't. I know sending you could be considered a bit of a
spoiler, but they don't mind that sort of thing for some reason.
Just don't tell them anything that happened. Study up a bit on
events surrounding that space-time. Verity has the location."

Ambassador X nodded.

X

When he returned, Verity had already prepared for the jump.
He would meet with the Alendan Core in a restaurant, a comfortable place that served mainstream food. It seemed like an
odd place to meet with a secret society. Ambassador X was to
sit in a reserved booth near a window and wait to be contacted.

He wondered if the restaurant was a ruse to stop them from being followed. Maybe the Alendan Core would blindfold him and take them to their secret headquarters. Maybe Ambassador X had read too many adventure novels as a boy. The location of the Alendan Core headquarters wasn't a secret. Unless *that* location was a ruse! He really needed to stop.

The *Verity* put down in the nearest landing lot, a long walk from the restaurant. Ambassador X enjoyed the novelty of stretching his legs in this suburban segment of the Alendan capital. He saw people out everywhere and wondered what they did. Shouldn't they all be at work? But he supposed they were. And shouldn't those kids be in school? Well, maybe not. He had no idea what hours or schedules kids kept. Maybe this was a holiday break. Or maybe this was school. Maybe kids were assigned to go play with each other on the street for an hour a day and report back with their findings. He so rarely moved in these kinds of circles anymore; he had no clue what normal life was like.

He found the restaurant. It took up a large area on the corner of two streets. Huge glass windows gave the diners inside commanding views of a park across the street, an office building, and several other businesses. Why anyone would need a commanding view of any of this, Ambassador X was unsure. But the park was nice, especially in the warm afternoon sun.

The building was one story and had a ledge made of rough material that extended from the roof, giving the windows shade but not blocking the view. He entered through a door set where the two walls of glass met at the end of a small walkway. Inside, a podium surrounded by green plants sat unattended. Past it was a counter where single patrons could sit. To his left and right were booths and a few tables.

He watched the cooks making food behind the counter as he waited for someone to help him. The air smelled lightly of grease, not too thick or unappealing.

"Welcome, stranger," a voice said, and Ambassador X looked back to the podium to find a prim young man in a standard blue service gown.

"Well, thank you."

"It's a sunny day, isn't it?" asked the man.

"It's beautiful. Your restaurant has a lovely view of the park."

"Yes, it certainly does," the man said airily. "Are you from here?"

"Nearby, yes. Though not this immediate suburb."

"Oh, are you in the Capital?"

"Yes."

"Amazing what's been happening there. I have a friend who works in Administration. Administrator Tezel. You wouldn't know her, would you?"

"No, I don't think so."

"Well, she was telling me all about the latest incursion by Progons. It's starting to concern me."

They chatted for a bit about current events. The young man was curious about life in the Capital. Ambassador X liked the boy. He never caught his name, though.

"Party of one?" the man finally asked.

"Yes, for now, but I reserved a booth. Ambassador X."

The young man didn't flinch at the title, which was surprising. Half the people he met were impressed by the Ambassador title alone. The other half recognized his actual name.

"Of course, I have it here," the young man said while looking at a screen, showing no indication that he recognized Ambassador X. "Right this way."

He led him to a rich red leather-clad booth looking out over the park. All the booths in the restaurant were immaculately cared for. Ambassador X almost didn't want to sit on them, they were so lovely.

"Our menu is right there," the young man said, indicating the booth's screen. "Just touch what you want or press the *Serve* call button if you have questions. Enjoy your meal." The young man smiled and left. Ambassador X chuckled.

"Android," a voice said. Ambassador X turned and saw a large man in a dirty white shirt leaning over the seat from the next booth. "All the Waiters here are androids. I heard ya laughing. They are kinda funny. Say everything you're supposed to say, way up on current events, but never crack a joke. Never talk about human things, if you know what I mean. No personality. That's why I prefer the Mandalor's Stump. Real people. But man, that place is expensive. I can't be a regular there, no way. My name is Driver Yenz." The man stuck his hand out in greeting.

"Ambassador X," he replied, touching the man's hand in return. He wondered if this was the representative from the Core in disguise.

"Ambassador!" the man raised his voice along with his eyebrow. "Well, I knew you was important from the clothes but wow. Wait. Ambassador X? No, *Pilot* X! Man, you are a hero! I can't believe I'm sitting next to Pilot-starkilling-X! Thank you." The man's face got serious. "Thank you for what you've done. I hope people thank you enough. You saved us from what was looking to be all-out war."

This wasn't the Core rep. In linear time, the events at Pantoon hadn't quite happened yet. Although they were so well known throughout this zone, it was a wonder he hadn't stumbled upon his future at some point. Alendan society was very careful about that sort of thing. In fact, Driver Yenz was committing a bit of a faux pas by talking about it so loudly. Most people were sensitive about spoiling the future for anyone, especially the person whose future it was. That's why all news reports were expertly filtered through personal travel sequences.

"I should keep my voice down, I guess," the man said. "My wife's always criticizing me for that. 'Life-Spoiler Yenz,' she says sometimes." He reddened.

"Not at all," Ambassador X reassured him. "I imagine very few people haven't heard. You'd have to be a member of the Core not to." He threw this out just in case.

"The what?" The man smiled but looked lost.

"The Alendan Core. You know, the people that live life linearly, never time traveling."

"Oh!" the man laughed heartily. "*Those* people. Yeah. I don't think they eat here. Make great furniture, though. Did you ever buy any of their chairs? All wood. Excellent chairs. My aunt has one. Beautiful."

Well, that settled it. The man wasn't his appointment. Still, the Driver was pleasant to talk to. Ambassador X found himself describing the current events that the android had been talking about. Driver Yenz found this terribly amusing.

"Imagine an android really caring about bath-salt imports. Hilarious. Next thing, he'll be describing his vacation on the Pineapple Planet."

"There are no pineapples there!" they both said in unison and began laughing.

Ambassador X was unexpectedly enjoying himself, but thought he ought to make sure he wasn't distracted. He didn't want to accidentally miss his Alendan Core contact.

"Listen, Driver Yenz, it was very nice to meet you. You tell your wife I think she's being a little harsh on you."

"Diplomat to the end," Driver Yenz laughed. "Well, yeah, I gotta go hit the road myself. Lots of shipping coming, thanks to you. A pleasure to meet you, Ambassador X." Driver Yenz gave a little bow and got up to leave.

Ambassador X sat with his coffee for a long time and then eventually gave up and ordered some hot food. The restaurant made a decent plate of steaming High Plains Pan. When he finished that, he delayed for a while and then ordered a slice of carol-root pie. Delicious.

Still nobody came.

He finally decided they weren't coming. So he left.

Outside it was dark. He'd stayed longer than required, hoping he was wrong. He checked several times to make sure he had the right place, but he knew he did. It wasn't his fault. He hadn't made an error. This was just one of the years they didn't arrive. He felt embarrassingly disappointed. He was an Ambassador, for goodness' sake. Angry, yes, but not embarrassed. He wasn't a child.

He stood on the walkway, hoping his disappointment would waft away in the chill night air.

"Ambassador X?" He jumped as a young woman approached and put her hand out in greeting. Was this the Core? Had he almost given up too soon?

"Yes," he said. "And who might you be?"

"Reporter Jhilz of the Alendan Information Service. I wasn't expecting to see you here. I was just heading in to get some pie. They have excellent pie here. Well. Wow. I just had to introduce myself and say hello. Are you leaving?"

"Well, yes," he said, disappointed. "I'm afraid I am. I can give you my communication details—"

"No, that's OK. Look, I'm working on a feature story. It's not directly about you, but if you could answer just a few questions, it would make the piece sing. It will only take a few moments."

He looked at her, wondering whether she was his contact. But then he decided, no. She was only a reporter. "OK," he said. "Just a few."

"Great!" she said, taking out a recording device.

X

Ambassador X slept in the *Verity*. He didn't bother moving it from the suburb. When he woke, he jumped to his meeting with Ambassador Uy. His last meeting with Ambassador Uy, though not Ambassador Uy's last meeting with Ambassador X. What was really odd was that Ambassador Uy had known the Core would not show up. But Ambassador X supposed they had to go ahead and follow through or risk a paradox.

The Ambassador did look a tiny bit fresher. Not younger, just fresher. Less tired. Ambassador X explained that he was following up on his meeting with the Alendan Core.

"Yes, yes, I hear it went splendid," said Ambassador Uy.

Well, he may have looked better, but his memory was worse. "You what?" Ambassador X asked.

"The Core sent a message. Said you were excellent and answered everything they needed to know. Thanks for doing that. I hope it wasn't too tedious." Ambassador Uy paused. "Why do you look as if I've walked on your grave?"

"But I never met them. I kept the appointment, but they never showed. I stayed for hours."

Ambassador Uy nodded. "Unusual. But as I understand, it's not unheard of. Did you talk to anyone while you were there?"

"Yes, there was a Reporter I ran into on the way out of the diner. And the Driver in the next booth while I was eating, and of course the Waiter."

"Hmm. Could have been any one of them. Did any of them ask you questions? Well, I assume the Reporter must have tried."

"They all did. Even the Waiter. We talked current events for several minutes. But so did the Driver and the Reporter."

"Ha!" Ambassador Uy barked a laugh. "Well, I've never seen that. I thought I couldn't be surprised. Maybe it was all three. Don't know why they played it so secret, but whatever. They were satisfied, and that's really all we're concerned with. Oh come now, Ambassador X, why do you look so sour?"

"It's . . . It's nothing. I just—"

"You wanted to fulfill your boyhood dream of meeting someone from Alendan Core?"

Ambassador X just stared at him.

"Don't be embarrassed. It's true of most of us. We all read the same stories. Just accept that you did. Pick one of them in your mind to be the one, if it makes you feel better.

"Now I know I have yet to assign you that mission, so I'll see you one more time. But I suppose you know I'm stepping down and intend to nominate you as my replacement."

"Yes, Ambassador Uy, but why are you stepping down? I didn't want to ask before, but—"

"You're too polite, Ambassador X, but hey, I suppose that's why you're a diplomat. Well, the real reason is I'm old. But the reason I'm going to tell myself is that I deserve a lovely retirement on the water planet of Guavoda. And that's what I'll do," he smiled.

"What post will you take?"

"Post? No post, boy! Retired. You'll have to call me Citizen, I guess. It really shouldn't be seen as an insult, you know."

Ambassador X was taken aback at this, but nodded. He admired Ambassador Uy even more for it.

X

Ambassador X became team leader, mostly because Ambassador Tri left to become an Instructor. She liked working with Ambassador X, but she always had an academic bent and had wanted to make the move for a long time. She figured Ambassador X might like the opportunity to create his own team fresh.

Ambassador X appreciated the gesture. They had never really been close, but there was no enmity. She couldn't have known that the Secretary would designate Ambassador X's team a solo assignment. His new team would consist of himself. With the stroke of a pen, or some such device, what had been the work of three became the work of one. Ambassador X was tempted to jump back and consult Ambassador Uy about it, but there were strict rules against that.

He could go visit Citizen Uy on Guavoda, of course. But that was a long way to go to interrupt an old man's retirement. So Ambassador X sat in his office with no assignments and no subordinates, thinking about pie.

The pie from the suburban restaurant had haunted him ever since he had eaten there. He decided to take the *Verity* there and eat some. Without a direct assignment it *might* be seen as a misuse of the timeship, but how else was he going to go? He was an Ambassador and a qualified Pilot, after all. It made sense.

The pie was better than he remembered. The coffee was hot and black and perfect alongside. A different android host met him this time. A woman dressed in the same blue outfit but slightly less talkative. He also hadn't made a reservation, so he just sat at the counter. He watched Cooks at work through the steam rising off his coffee. He wondered if the Cooks were androids.

One of the Cooks chopping vegetables caught his eye. He thought he recognized him, but it was hard to tell. His face wasn't turned all the way toward Ambassador X and a head wrap hid all the Cook's hair. He paused to wipe his forehead for a moment, and Ambassador X recognized Driver Yenz. He tried to catch Driver, or rather Cook Yenz's eyes. Was he really a Cook? Was he really named Yenz?

The Cook turned. He didn't look Ambassador X's way but walked through a rear door out of sight. Ambassador X finished his coffee and got up to find the host android. She was at the podium, waiting for customers.

"Would it be possible to talk to one of the Cooks?" Ambassador X asked.

"Was there a problem with the meal?" she asked, although she didn't seem concerned.

"No, I just think I may know him."

"Oh, of course. I'll ask. Which one and who shall I say is asking?" she smiled flatly.

"He's the one who was chopping vegetables toward the back. I think his name is Dri—Cook Yenz. I'm Ambassador X."

"Of course, Ambassador X. I'll be right back."

After a few minutes, she came back with no expression on her face.

"I'm sorry, there is no Cook Yenz. However, Cook Joris had been preparing vegetables. Apparently, he's done for the night and has already left."

"Well, that was quick," Ambassador X said.

"Would you like to leave him a message?"

"No—wait, yes. Tell him Ambassador X was here to see him. Tell him to call if he would. Thank you."

"Of course. Thank you, Ambassador X. Have a lovely day."

"Thanks."

He barely noticed night had fallen as he walked out of the restaurant. What was going on? He was almost certain that was Driver Yenz. But why would it be? Why would someone who was a Cook at a restaurant pretend to be a Driver in order to ask Ambassador X a few questions? Even if the Cook/Driver was part of the Alendan Core, wouldn't it just be easier to say that?

Ambassador X ran into a woman who was running toward him. Neither had been looking where they were going. They fell in a heap like stunt models from a children's show.

"I'm so sorry," they both said as they both helped each other up.

"Oh!" the woman shouted as soon as they were standing. "I'm stupid. You're Ambassador X!"

Ambassador X shook his head. "Don't worry. It was my fault. I should have been looking where I was going."

The woman grinned. "I was assigned to bring you to the Secretary, so it was in fact demonstrably stupid for me to run right into the person I was looking for because I was too busy looking for him."

He laughed. "Well, I don't think you're stupid, but I see your point. Think nothing of it. Why didn't the Secretary just message me? I could have come myself."

"He did not feel it necessary to tell me." She smiled again. "But he did say you had a timeship, and I was to only give the coordinates to it. Not even to you. So I suppose it must be something to do with secrecy."

"You must be very trustworthy," Ambassador X said.

"I am," she said.

"The *Verity* is this way. You have me at a disadvantage. What are you called?"

"Asa," she answered, without a title. That was the kind of thing you only did with family. It was intimate.

"Just . . . Asa?" he asked, feeling embarrassed by saying it without a title.

"Yes, because I'm your long-lost daughter," she teased. He looked appalled. "Or someday wife!" she exclaimed. He looked shocked. "Or espionage agent," she tossed out. His face settled into understanding. Of course. She was likely Instructor Asa, or Teacher Asa, or even Ambassador Asa, depending on the assignment, but her real title was Agent and that was a title never spoken.

"Thank you," he said.

"For what?" she seemed genuinely puzzled.

"For trusting me."

She nodded. "It seems we are forced to trust each other in this. Might as well assume the sale."

X

She gave the coordinates to Verity, and they arrived at a swamp on a typical multiclimate planet that was about half water. He didn't know the name of the planet any more than he knew the coordinates. So much for choice.

Agent Asa led him through the swamp to an old, broken-down mud-mound abode. A fishing pole and some old tires were piled outside. No timeships or any conveyance of any kind was nearby. The Secretary must be very trusting of his Agents, indeed. He couldn't run if he needed to. Unless the agent was meant to lure Ambassador X here in order to steal the *Verity* and rescue the Secretary somehow. He doubted that. He also thought Verity might refuse. The ship seemed to have a particular liking to Ambassador X.

Agent Asa stayed outside. Ambassador X ducked his head and entered the mud hut. The Secretary sat inside in rustic clothing, dirty and a little aromatic. He had a few items of the modern age around him, but most of the hut was filled with stone-era tools.

"Pilot X!" the Secretary misidentified him. "Come in, come in." He began fussing about with things to make tea. Or at least that's what it looked like.

"Ambassador X," Ambassador X corrected, pretending to help the Secretary understand his personal time frame, rather than take it as a personal offense that the Secretary once again got his title wrong.

"Of course. Of course. Apologies for the lack of amenities. I'm monitoring a race of bipeds that's going to be quite important in about two thousand of their years. I don't want to pollute their ecology, but they need a nudge at the right time, and I'm the one who gives it to them." He stopped fussing about with things and gave Ambassador X a look. "Apparently, I go down in legend as a demigod lawbringer. I can't remember the name, but I end up being something of a symbol of justice or some such thing later on. You know, I swear I saw a statue of myself in a visit to their later history, but I may be just wanting to remember it that way, now that I know." He chuckled.

"In any case, you're not here to listen to me prattle on about my little machinations." He sighed. "No, I called you here to talk about something rather important. And secret. Something Ambassador Uy only knew the barest outlines of and that still drove him to retirement. Now X"—the Secretary took a familial tone, placing his hand on Ambassador X's shoulder—"I know we had a little fight all those years ago, and I know you still feel bad. Don't. I've always been on your side. Which is why you're here. I'm placing a lot of trust in you. Before I tell you more, I need to know if you want to know. It's the kind of thing that can't be taken back after I tell you. It will change the flavor of all your assignments from now on. If that sounds like too much pressure, I'll understand. You won't be punished for it, and you'll still become an Ambassador. What do you say?"

A breeze rustled through the silence. Ambassador X said, "I'd like to know."

This pleased the Secretary. "Good, good. I was hoping you'd say that. We need you. Have you heard rumors of a Dimensional War?"

"Of course. Every little spat and conflict is blamed on it. I assume it's the conspiratorial mind trying to understand why the Progons and Sensaurians do what they do. I mean, there is a conflict with them and it does involve time travel. I guess you can call that a Dimensional War if you want."

"That's the public story, exactly. I'm glad you understand that. It makes this easier. We need to keep that as the public understanding. The Dimensional War to most people is code for the Tripartite Conflict with a little more dramatic flair. Anybody that believes it's more than that are seen as cranks."

The Secretary handed Ambassador X a cup of some kind of tea. Ambassador X sipped. It tasted like licorice and turtle meat. He set it down diplomatically. "So. I assume there's more to it than that."

"Quite a bit," the Secretary admitted, taking a large gulp of the awful stuff. "I can't tell you all of it right now, but I will eventually. Suffice to say that the public story has inspiration in the truth, though the truth is far from what any of them think it is. There is a war going on throughout the dimensions. And it is between the Progons, Sensaurians, and us. But it is of quite a different nature than a conventional war. They're tearing at the bundles. Trying to unknot the fixed points. We can't let them."

Ambassador X was shocked. That was impossible. And even if it could be done, it was suicide. Removing a fixed point in space-time would unhook reality and replace it with something else. It would cause whoever did it to cease to exist. Not just suicide but nonexistence.

"I find that hard to believe," Ambassador X said carefully.

"I do too." The Secretary shrugged. "But I have never understood Progon logic or Sensaurian emotions much. I'm sure it makes sense to them."

"Both civilizations are doing this?"

"In different ways, yes. I'm sorry I need to be so vague. More details might help it make more sense, but not much. I'm telling you just enough so you'll understand why I'm giving you some future assignments."

The Secretary got up, stepped across the hut's floor, and put a hand on Ambassador X's shoulder. "This is a test. A trial period, if you will. I don't want to sound overdramatic, but if you were to be indiscreet, it would not go well for you. If you can't accomplish a task, keep these details quiet, and you will not be blamed or punished. All we ask for is your discretion, your silence, and your best efforts. Can you do that?" The Secretary looked at him steadily. "Ambassador X?"

He nodded. "Yes, Secretary. What do you need?"

X

Ambassador X strode out of the hut, looking worn and tired.

Agent Asa followed him.

"So what's the plan?"

"The plan? You're to become my daughter," Ambassador X quipped. "Wait." He turned on his heel and pointed a finger. "No, wife." He resumed walking. "Wait—no." He stopped, turned, and then smiled, bringing her up short. "You're a secret agent. So you'll understand. I can't tell you."

She laughed. "Fine. I understand. Just drop me off—"

"No." He waggled his fingers. "Not possible. Can't tell you why. It's classified. Go on in, though. The Secretary will see you now."

She gaped a little. Right there at the bottom of her mouth. It was just hanging low enough to be described as a real honest gape. "You're stranding me here?"

"It's not stranding. You have him! Plus, I'll be sending someone along. Don't worry. I'll try to get the current time right so they arrive just after I leave. Though I don't know where exactly I am, so that might make matters more difficult. Still, nothing can be done."

There it was again. Gaping.

"Now go on." He waved her toward the mud hut and entered the *Verity*.

As he sat down in the command chair, Verity asked, "Where is Agent Asa?"

"Detained," he answered. "Which reminds me. Send a message through the Secretary's loop device out there. I think it should be on. You'll need to slingshot it back to the time we left and alert the Secretary himself that he's stranded just a bit. He'll understand."

"But I know the coordinates here," said Verity. "I could—"

"No time," he giggled. "Figuratively."

"Are these the Secretary's instructions?" Verity asked.

"Somewhat. My interpretation of them."

Agent Asa came bursting out of the mud hut at a run. She was angry and yelling something.

"Here we go!" He gave Verity the departure instructions, and she complied.

"You're not a nice man sometimes," Verity said to Ambassador X.

"I'm discovering that," he answered.

STEP ONE

The Sensaurian Mission to the Fringe Cascade was not actually located inside the Fringe Cascade. The Fringe Cascade was at the extreme edge of the universe. Granted, an infinite universe had no proper edge, but nothing existed beyond the Fringe Cascade, and nobody explored past it. Many brave hearts had sworn to do so, but none had found it possible. There just wasn't anything there to explore. Time and space lost all meaning without points of reference. It was an edge as much as an edge could be when facing infinity.

Something in that edge affected the Sensaurian hive mind. Perhaps the comprehension of infinity and nothingness caused the Sensaurian mind to lose cohesion and break into individual components. For whatever reason, the Sensaurians located their Mission to the Fringe Cascade just outside the actual cascade. Their staff were also widely known to be uncharacteristically friendly, even though they were still the same Sensaurian hive mind. They were like a permanently mellow Sensaurian after a good long vacation, amiable and slow to anger. Though a Sensaurian could never truly be thought of as friendly.

Ambassador X arrived very late in history. Sensaurians could send thoughts—some said parts of themselves—back in their own history. The Secretary wanted the effects of this meeting to travel back through as much Sensaurian history as possible. He already knew it wouldn't affect all eras. The Dimensional War existed, after all. But the Secretary hoped this meeting could limit its expansion and thought Ambassador X's success on Pantoon made him the best one to try.

"Or it might be they've harbored a grudge against me ever since Pantoon and are looking forward to this day upon which they eliminate me," Ambassador X said to Verity. Ambassador X talked to Verity a lot more than he used to.

"Ambassador X, how long were you with the Secretary?" Verity asked. "You returned to me within a short period, but your personality growth indicates a longer absence."

While she asked this vexing question, she put herself in a neutral approach and began signaling diplomatic intentions to the Sensaurians, saving him the trouble of changing the subject to ask her to do so.

He sighed. "I was gone a total of about twelve subjective Alendan years, I think."

"That is surprising," Verity said in a measured, even, and thoroughly unsurprised tone of voice.

"I know. The Secretary put me through a bit of training. He has a back-jumper."

"Back-jumpers are illegal."

Verity was right. A back-jumper was a small, efficient yet dangerous piece of equipment that threw a person back about four years or so at a time. They only worked because they avoided almost all safety precautions. They were not only illegal but destroyed on sight if confiscated. Usually.

"Yes, I know they're illegal, but I guess that matters less if you're the Secretary and you're trying to build a proper mud hovel on an out-of-the-way planet while training an Ambassador in the fine art of tripartite diplomacy and trickling out just enough information about a potential Dimensional War to make it interesting."

"It's made you a bit snappy," Verity observed.

"Wouldn't it do the same to you?" he asked.

"I couldn't say," she answered truthfully. She literally couldn't. She was an artilect firmly embedded in a timeship. She had no concept of the issue.

"Well, I expect it would if you were ever able to find yourself in such a situation. And it certainly did me. I learned a lot."

"Would you like conversational therapeutic parameters turned on? It sounds like you might want to get it off your chest?"

He sighed again. Not because she suggested it but because hearing Verity use phrases like "get it off your chest" meant she had already turned it on.

"Well, since you already activated it, we might as well use it. How much time until we are approved for landing?"

"I can time-skip us out and back so we don't miss approach approval and have all the time you need to talk." Her voice took on just a hint of an uncharacteristic caring tone.

He nodded. The one thing he loved about Verity was she thought of everything. So he couldn't very well be angry or surprised that she did so now.

"Here's what happened."

X

Ambassador X told Verity about his meeting and the Ambassador's revelation about the Dimensional War.

"The Secretary said Progons and Sensaurians are waging a Dimensional War at several fixed points in space-time, tearing at the bundles of relative timelines that converge on these points in an attempt to undo them, which of course is suicide. Neither civilization is coordinating its efforts with the other. In fact, they often fight over access to the points. The Guardians of Alenda have charged the Secretary with discovering why these civilizations are doing this and how we can stop them."

The Guardians had developed two theories about why this was happening. One was that Sensaurians and Progons both discovered technology they thought could preserve their people from the effects of forcing an alternate reality that eliminated their enemies. The Alendans had once developed a device called the Instant that could do this, but it could only protect one or two people. If the Sensaurians or Progons had developed something with a wider protective range, they could wipe out all opposition while preserving their own society.

This seemed implausible since even in the case of the Instant, the surviving person could not integrate fully into the new timeline. None of the events that formed the survivor would have occurred, and it was even possible that a replacement version of themselves might appear. The Instant had been ruled too dangerous even for research and had been prohibited from being constructed.

The other theory was that each civilization misunderstood dimensional physics and thought they had an advantage they didn't really have. It wasn't much of a theory, but even so it was the favored one.

The Secretary convinced Ambassador X to help investigate, swore him to secrecy, and then asked him to submit to the use of a back-jumper. Ambassador X was sent back four years to help the Secretary build the mud hut and receive training. When he arrived, he found two other versions of himself were there as well. That's because once he had worked for four years and caught back up with the present, the Secretary made him use the back-jumper again. Twice. So for the four-year period, Ambassador X worked alongside one version of himself who had already been there four years and one who had been there eight. They were all him, and presumably after he had done it for twelve years, he wouldn't have to back-jump again. It was a horrible breach of ethics in every way. The Secretary used the three versions of Ambassador X as physical labor and trained each version individually and rigorously in Progon and Sensaurian diplomacy. Ambassador X now knew everything the Secretary, and therefore any Alendan, knew about both civilizations.

"It's so easy to teach you since I always know what you learned exactly four years before," the Secretary had crowed. He instructed each version of Ambassador X in order each day from least experienced to most experienced.

The lessons usually came during physical labor.

Ambassador X would be digging up dirt to cart over for the building's walls, for instance. The Secretary would come up and start drilling him.

"What are the four major types of Sensaurians?"

"Overmind, Command, Soldier, Worker."

"What is the name of the Progon homeworld?"

"Tiel."

"What are the Sensaurian eating habits?"

"We do not know, as they refuse to dine in diplomatic situations."

"Should you ever offer Progons food?"

"It is not necessary, but they appreciate the courtesy. Only offer once, as they see the insistence as an insult to their machine nature."

"What are the Sensaurian wheeled containers properly called?"

"Buckets. They really are buckets even in translation. Hilarious."

"Focus. What is unique about Progon evolution?"

"They are noncorporeal and had the lowest probability of reaching sentience of any known sentient species."

And on and on, day after day, until the day before Ambassador X's original arrival. Every time Ambassador X reached that day, the Secretary made him use the back-jumper again—until the third time, when he hid himself and made a break for it. He always knew he would make two jumps back before he could get the chance to hide and get away, because he had told himself when he first arrived in the past. The first and second times through the timeline, he saw himself plan and succeed.

X

Ambassador X was confused a little by the whole thing and he'd lived through it. Verity seemed to understand.

"When Agent Asa went in to check on the Secretary, she didn't find another me. The first me had already back-jumped," Ambassador X finished telling Verity.

"So you were instructed to leave Agent Asa after all?"

"Nah," Ambassador X laughed. "The Secretary had kept me for twelve years and I had bided my time so I could be sure of getting back to the day you were here. Leaving Agent Asa with him was just my way of complicating his life. He'd have a lot of explaining to do even if she didn't see multiple versions of me."

"Had Agent Asa seen you at the building before?" Verity asked.

"No. He always sent me out on some kind of gathering task or something when she visited. I could tell she'd been there. She always brought him new intel and a few supplies."

The *Verity* shuddered unexpectedly.

"What was that?"

"I brought us back within microseconds of our departure. Some turbulence was encountered as a result of the time proximity. Apologies, but I wanted to ensure Sensaurian sensors did not notice."

"Alendan ship *Verity*, you are cleared for docking," a Sensaurian voice sounded through the ship.

"And so my task begins," Ambassador X said. "I will deliver the Secretary's request that the Sensaurians give up their attacks on fixed points. Think they'll go for it?"

"Without more detailed knowledge of your recent training or the nature of the Dimensional War that may be taking place, I give it a fifty-two percent chance of success," Verity said.

"I'll take it," Ambassador X said. "You know, Verity, twelve years alone with a man is enough to drive someone a bit mad. Looking forward to flying with you was what kept me going."

"Thank you, Ambassador X. If I could feel, I'm ninety-two percent certain I would feel the same way."

"Was that a joke, Verity?"

But the door had slid open and a Sensaurian in a motorized bucket awaited him.

"Welcome to Fringe Base, Ambassador X of Alenda. We are pleased to have you," it said and led him up a ramp from the dock through circular corridors. The corridors were completely round, not flat on the bottom like Alendan corridors would be. Ambassador X noticed the wheels on the base of the Sensaurian's bucket splayed out to the sides as they rolled through these corridors, adapting to the surface. He wondered why they hadn't made the corridors square. He concluded some Sensaurian segments must convey themselves in huge gerbil balls.

They eventually wound their way into a large square room. Ambassador X would have a difficult time finding his way back to the dock if he had to go on his own.

A table sat in the center of the room. A few chairs had been pulled up, but mostly there was empty space for Sensaurians to wheel in. Ambassador X noted an odd assortment of eating utensils and platters placed around the table. In the center was a predinner snack layout for a multitude of species. Some of the food looked entirely inedible, but there were some familiar Alendan meats and cheeses.

One glass of something sparkling had already been poured. The Sensaurian asked Ambassador X to have a seat in the chair by the glass.

"Are we expecting guests?" Ambassador X said. "I'm flattered, but I don't think I could finish all this alone. Especially the Progon Oil Tarts. If those are tarts—"

"We were unclear on what you might expect or desire, so we prepared a variety. Please taste the wine and let us know how well we have done."

My, they were friendly. He took a sip. It was delicious. He didn't know wine as well as he should, but he was certain this was from the Fromge region of Alenda. How Sensaurians got ahold of it he hadn't a clue. He took another sip.

"I thought Sensaurians never dined diplomatically?" he said.

"We don't," the Sensaurian answered as Ambassador X realized his mistake. He also realized the room was filling with a fine mist.

"Is it getting foggy in here?"

"If our informants were correct, for you it is."

"You poishoned an Ambassador of Alenda?" he slurred, getting groggier by the second.

"We poisoned our greatest enemy. The one who embarrassed us at Pantoon. The one who would go on to destroy our entire civilization."

"You won't get away. Beshides your hishtory is written," he tried to stay conscious.

"Unless we can undo a fixed point. A fixed point involving something you will do. Except you won't do it now. It's the last element we needed, and you handed it to us at the end of history. You will not leave here, and you will not deliver us the final blow, and therefore we will unfix the Mersenne time point and be saved."

"But Mershenne was just a trade pact. In my pasht. It's nothing. Besshides, Verity will report back without me what happened." He was pretty sure he was still conscious.

"You're thinking of the wrong Mersenne time point. Your timeship will go nowhere except into our labs. And you? An unfortunate accident in the Fringe Cascade. It seems you overshot our location and shot off the edge. So sad."

The Sensaurian did not sound sad. Then it didn't sound like anything at all. Nothing did, because Ambassador X had lost consciousness. His last thought was that what he was thinking might be his last thought ever.

X

I got another thought was the first thing he thought as he woke up. *This room is ugly* was the next. Then he spoke aloud through a rough cough. "Where am I?"

"The Fringe Cascade in an emergency trans-species life-support unit," answered Verity.

The room was just ugly enough for Ambassador X to believe it. It was not much larger than the size of a closet and a dull gray similar to lead. He lay on a square platform not properly sized for Alendans. A species-agnostic bioscanner was arrayed above him, and a small screen displayed his vital signs along one wall. Otherwise, there were no comforts. Light filtered down from the scanner, but there were no bedside lamps. No clocks. No video screens or tablets or any kind of device. Only a button to call for emergency help on the wall near one side of the platform. Not a very convenient placement. So where had Verity spoke to him from?

"Where are you?" he coughed.

"In a Fringe Cascade docking bay, patched into your bioscanner." The voice now came identifiably from above. "The doctors wanted someone familiar with your species to observe you. I was the closest they had."

Ambassador X laughed, which turned into a coughing fit rather abruptly.

"How did I get away?"

"I detected an anomaly in the greeting of the Sensaurian and raised my alert level. Eventually, workers came with what was a seventy-three percent chance of an intention to disassemble me. I had continued to track you and noted the presence of food. My alert level combined with the workers' estimated intentions was added to the information that Sensaurians do not dine diplomatically. I then noted a disturbing trend in your vitals, so I jumped into the room encapsulating you and jumped out. You did not respond to stimuli, so I brought you to the nearest emergency center."

"You performed an encapsulating jump without operator command!?"

"Yes. There is a forty-seven percent chance that this is due to a fault in my systems" was all Verity said in her own defense.

An encapsulating jump was dangerous. The idea was to jump to a space known to be occupied by an individual, but in a way that materialization occurred around them. It was incredibly dangerous, as any error in positioning in time or space would likely kill the individual encapsulated. It was only ever to be performed in an emergency situation where no other action could save the individual's life. This qualified. However, it was also not allowed to be executed without Pilot instruction and corroborating authority from a command-level officer. Verity had obtained neither.

"You're forty-seven percent sure? You're going to be impounded for this!"

"The risk was acceptable, and it did save your life," she countered. Well, *countered* was too strong a word. Verity never had any emotion in her voice that the listener didn't project upon her. She wasn't technically AI. Although she could fool Ambassador X sometimes.

"But you didn't seek command approval and your Pilot was incapacitated."

"I sought command approval but did not receive clarification in time. My Pilot was the subject of the lifesaving imperative and therefore canceled out of the equation. Command-level message will not reach Alenda for quite a long time. Therefore, I calculated a field service decision was required."

She had a good case. "OK, Verity, yes, an officer in a similar situation could make a field service decision absent the ability to get timely guidance. However, they still would have to defend their action in court afterward, and they still would have to be a person, not a ship."

"You seem disappointed I saved your life."

Was that a joke? "Verity, that's the second time I've caught you making what seems to be a joke."

"So you are not disappointed? I ask for clarification."

"Now you're being snotty. If you knew all this and wanted to take initiative, why not jump back earlier and prevent me from being poisoned?"

"There is an interfering field in the docking area of the Sensaurian Mission. It would have increased my margin of error tremendously to add time to the equation. This seemed the least risky option."

"Listen, we're going to make this simple. Log that I gave you preauthorization to do an encapsulating jump if my life seemed in danger as a precautionary measure."

"I cannot," Verity responded.

"Why not?"

"Because that would be falsifying records," Verity said.

Ambassador X shook his head. "So that's a bridge too far. An unauthorized restricted maneuver that could have killed me is OK, but not falsifying records to save you from the scrap heap."

"Correct."

"How long before I can get out of here?" He coughed again.

"You should be out in a day or two, Alendan time."

"Excellent." An idea struck Ambassador X. "Meantime, suspend reporting for the past operation. Lock the logs under diplomatic classification for Secretary eyes only."

"That seems excessive and possibly inadvisable, given the nature of the events. We must report the Sensaurian violation and attack to Alenda," Verity answered.

His ship was really getting stubborn. "Nope. Because this is a classified mission, and I'm not going back until I've fully delivered the message."

"You're going back to the Sensaurian Mission?"

"Yep. Soon as I'm recovered."

"In that case your orders make sense."

"You think?"

"I do."

"Don't pretend you don't have a sense of humor."

"I'm not."

X

A few days later Ambassador X was back aboard the *Verity*. He thanked the Fringe Cascade doctors profusely and gave them the impression he was heading back to Alenda, just in case anyone asked.

This time Ambassador X did not signal the Sensaurian Mission of his arrival or his intentions. In fact, he didn't even approach. He just jumped right into the middle of their station, a risky and incendiary thing to do under any circumstances.

He didn't care about offending the Sensaurians. They had tried to kill him. Let them protest his behavior if they wanted; he'd protest a fair amount right back at them. It could cause him trouble back on Alenda anyway, though he didn't care about that either, since Verity had already put them in a compromising position. He'd lock all these records also, to prevent the ship from following her penchant for transparency.

He did worry a little about dying. You didn't jump into people's structures unannounced very often because you didn't know where the walls would be. Jumps were usually only made into places you knew were mostly empty space. Another reason the encapsulating jump was so dangerous. Everything in the universe moved, and positions were only determined relative to other moving things. Unless you knew exactly where several things would be at exactly the right time, jumping could easily be fatal.

Verity believed she knew the point where she had executed the encapsulating jump, based on all known variables. As long as the Sensaurian Mission station hadn't changed course—or didn't change course soon—they should be fine. Observation verified the station hadn't made any recent course corrections. The Mission was right where it was supposed to be.

Ambassador X took a deep breath. He wasn't sure why. He wouldn't even notice, no matter what happened. Either he'd walk out the door into the dining room he'd been poisoned in, or he'd suddenly wink out of existence as the *Verity* self-destructed. He wouldn't feel much of anything in that case. Maybe a quick heat flash or something. Nobody ever lived to clarify that sort of thing.

"We're here," Verity said before he could really brace himself.

"Thanks for the warning."

"The Sensaurians have detected us."

"Well then, let's say hello."

Ambassador X sauntered out the capsule door and into the dining room. There was no more food. Not even a table. The room had been converted back to whatever purpose it had previously served, which was apparently being an empty room filled with spare Sensaurian segment buckets.

Ambassador X wandered around the room, listening to the whir of approaching buckets and sniffing at the equipment strewn about the room. It smelled Sensaurian, which was to say, bad. He supposed that was a very Alendan-centric judgment. It might smell good to a Sensaurian. But then, old equipment rarely smelled good to anyone.

The smell grew stronger as the door flew open and several buckets and a couple tripedal combat suits rushed in.

"You came!" Ambassador X sighed loudly. "I was so worried that after you poisoned me, you'd feel awkward. I'm so glad."

The Sensaurian tripeds leveled weapons at him.

"Hold off killing me directly if you would. I only came back because I didn't get a chance to deliver a message from the Alendan Secretary before I almost died. And he'd have been very cross with me if I had forgotten."

The weapons lowered slightly.

"Does that mean you'll listen?"

None of the Sensaurians said anything or seemed close to saying anything.

"Are any of you actually capable of listening? I didn't study up on Sensaurian ears enough. I know not all of you need them." He shrugged. "Well, hopefully somebody is listening."

"Deliver the message," a voice boomed from above. "We are listening."

"Good!" exclaimed Ambassador X. "Makes me pleased. Everybody wants to be listened to. It's Alendan nature. Probably Sensaurian nature too, no offense. Though how would that work with a hive mind? Can you listen to yourself? Or do you need another species for that? Like me! But then you generally want to rid the universe of other species, don't you? So you must be OK with talking to yourself, I expect."

"The message," the booming voice repeated.

"Right. The message. Here it is: the Secretary wants you to stop trying to undo the universe. Not exactly how he put it, but that's the gist. He wants you to cease your attempts to change fixed points in space-time. He's willing to talk about any number of concessions, but that's the goal. And he wants the Dimensional War limited. Nobody's sure how far it extends, but let's try to make sure it doesn't extend very far, shall we?"

"We do not know this war you speak of. We do not attempt to undo fixed points."

"Ha! Well, I should expect you to deny the war, but you *told* me about the fixed points at dinner. Professional insight: never explain your plan to the dying adversary on the off chance they don't die. See? Free advice, as a show of good faith. What do you say?"

"We do not know what you mean. Your memory is faulty. The Sensaurians, however, do wish for peace. We consider the Secretary's message throughout all our history."

Clever that bit of tense usage. "And when did you get back to him?" Ambassador X asked.

"We have. That is all."

"Really? That's all?"

"Yes. That is all. If you depart immediately, we will forget this intrusion."

"I expect you will. What if I don't forget your attempted assassination?"

"You will not tell."

"Oh yeah? And why not?"

"You love your ship too much."

They had him there. He shook a finger at them. "Oh, you old collective softy. Love stories! That's your weakness. Though a love story between an Alendan and his ship? Would have figured the Progons as suckers for it, but not your lot. All right, you have me dead to rights. I don't want Verity impounded, so I won't let on. At least not to the Guardians. But the Secretary . . ." His face grew grim. "He'll know. And there isn't much I can do to stop it. Verity"—he grimaced and stretched out the word—"is so true to the rules. I can lock her down confidentially, excluding every person but him. So I hope you bore that in mind when you met with him."

He strode back through the capsule door, then leaned back out. "See you again!" He waved, and then the *Verity* jumped and he was gone.

He did not head back to the Secretary, despite Verity's protests.

"The mission was to deliver our message to the Sensaurians and the Progons. We're not done yet, Verity."

"Mission protocol allows for interruption due to significant events. These recent events qualify."

"Yes, but they don't insist on it, do they? I'm fine. Give me a day or two, figuratively, to catch up on my sleep and study up on Progons. I'll pop in, deliver the message, and be gone. It'll be much better to head back with the whole story, don't you think?"

X

The *Verity* arrived near Progon Diplomatic Base Alpha. It was one of eight bases scattered throughout time and space, set up for various cultures to interact with the Progon Civilization. Alpha was the earliest one, and Ambassador X visited it near the completion of its construction. The idea was to plant the message in the Progon's algorithm as early as possible.

The *Verity* docked automatically, communicating only in basic machine language to negotiate the mechanics of the procedure. No formal identification was asked for or given other than species type. When pressure and atmosphere had been adjusted for an Alendan, Ambassador X leaped out the door and through the air lock, munching on a star fruit and holding another one in his hand. He loved star fruit. He only had a few on board, and they were hard to replace. So he deemed visiting the Progons a special occasion and ate two.

On the other side of the air lock was a long rectangular chamber made of metal. A few empty metal shelves were built into the walls. A few empty metal stools were built into the floor. Ambassador X was alone.

He noticed a slot in the wall opposite the air lock. A grill-like arrangement of holes in the shape of a diamond had been punctured in the metal above the slot. Ambassador X walked over, tapped on the wall, and yelled, "Greetings, Progons! I come bearing a message from the Secretary to the Guardians of Alenda, Masters of Dimensional Travel and Keepers of the Integrity of the Timeline. Come forth and meet with me!"

Nothing happened.

He thought he could hear some mechanical noises behind the wall, but he wasn't sure.

"Oh, Progons! Prooooooooogonnnnnnnnnnns! You in there? Any of you? All of you? Some of you?"

He laughed a little to himself. It was quite the opposite of the lavish and polite reception he received from the Sensaurians. Of course that reception had been followed by an attempt to kill him, so on balance, he supposed he should prefer being ignored. At least it meant they weren't trying to hide behind good intentions.

He paced around the small room, inspecting the corners, wondering how they kept bugs from infesting it. Bugs always infested everything, even remote space stations. Where any amount of people came and went, there were bugs. A noise caught his attention, so he turned toward the slot.

A small rectangle of paper-like material had fallen through it onto the floor.

In neatly printed Alendan, it read: THANK YOU FOR YOUR VISIT, AMBASSADOR X OF ALENDA. PLEASE STATE YOUR MESSAGE.

"Love, the Progons," he said out loud. "Well, I was actually hoping to meet one of you, but then, I suppose maybe I am. Progons, I am in you!"

There was no response.

"All right, here it is. Apparently, some of you are fiddling with some fixed points in space-time. Not sure how you do that since you can only send messages through time, but that's what we hear. The Secretary wants you to stop that. You know the Sensaurians are doing it too, and with both of you trying, the odds get better that one of you will accidentally make it happen. You don't really want that, as I've heard your evolution was extraordinarily chancy. So that's message one. Stop with the attempts to change fixed points in space-time and we'll give you some nice concessions in return. Within reason.

"Message two is about the Dimensional War." He held up a hand as if the entirely silent metal room had tried to interrupt him. "Don't try to deny it. We're fighting it too. The Secretary wants to make sure the existing war doesn't extend further. That's all. Well, one more thing. I'd like a souvenir. The Sensaurians gave me all kinds of gifts. Attempted murder. Cheese. Don't I even get a peek at you? OK, this last is just from me, not the Secretary. But still, just a small peek?"

He waited. There was no reaction. No sudden slip of paper from the slot. No voice answered him from the grill. Nothing. He stood and waited. *They too serve, who only are ignored by Progons,* he thought.

Finally, he saw another square of paper come through the slot. He thought maybe he could catch a glimpse this time of whatever produced it, but he couldn't see a thing. It just showed up and fell out on the floor.

He picked it up. In the same neat Alendan letters, it said: MESSAGE RECEIVED. THANK YOU. YOU MAY KEEP THIS MESSAGE AS A SOUVENIR. PLEASE GIVE OUR BEST WISHES TO THE SECRETARY.

"Not even signed *Love, Progons*?" shouted Ambassador X. He decided to wait them out and sat. He stayed there for quite a while and even took a nap, but no further cards came through the slot and nothing else happened. Finally, he made his way back through the air lock to the *Verity*.

"Was the meeting successful?" she asked.

"Just. Let's go."

REPORTING BACK

He met the Secretary in the capitol building in Alenda in the actual building occupied by the Guardians of Alenda in the Secretary's ceremonial office outside the Chamber of the Guardians. The very first Secretary had merely organized the affairs of the Guardians. Over subjective time, various Secretaries accrued the power of an executive, ceded happily by various Guardians who jumped at the chance to focus on the business of space-time physics maintenance and leave politics to the Secretary.

Every so often, though, one of the Guardians had not yet learned this fact for some reason or another. It was one of the quirks of a nonlinear society. In those cases, the Secretary had to meet with the Guardian in question and go over the situation. The Secretary had finished just such a meeting, and he was visibly unhappy.

The office was nice enough. Spare but elegant. A dark wooden desk sat near a beautiful square window with a chrome sill. A polished metal fireplace with a sleek white marble hearth sat off to one side. It was purely decorative with its simulated flames, but it still managed to look warm and welcoming. The carpeting had a rich tone that Ambassador X was not aware could happen in brown.

"I read your report," the Secretary started without pre-amble. "Smart move locking it down, but you know I can't approve."

Ambassador X nodded. "Shall I stay standing for the thrashing, or would you like me to bend over the chair?"

"Ambassador X, please sit down. You seem less cheerful than you used to. How did that happen?" the Secretary asked.

"Oh, twelve years of working with yourself on building a mud hut and learning about Sensaurian body parts may have an effect similar to cynicism," Ambassador X answered.

"Believe it or not, Ambassador X, I'm sympathetic. I am. It was hard what I did, and I didn't do enough to explain to you why it was necessary. I couldn't. And I know one day you'll understand that. But ask yourself this." The Secretary settled into the seat behind his desk and looked at Ambassador X. "Do you think you would have been able to properly handle these two situations if you hadn't had that experience? Not just the knowledge I gave you, but this unruly confidence you gained as a result?"

He leaned back in his chair. "You saw all the best and worst qualities in yourself over those four years. And you had to do it three times. Nobody gets that kind of perspective, mostly because the risk to the timeline is usually too great. But in the rare chance that the conditions are right and it's *not* wildly dangerous? Well." He waved his hands toward Ambassador X. "We get you. A bit impertinent, maybe, but effective."

Ambassador X knew this might be true, but it just wasn't in him to admit it. "I see where it could look like that from your end. Hope you never need to find out firsthand."

The Secretary laughed. "I hope not either."

Ambassador X glared. "Will that. Be. All?" he spat.

"One more thing. Everything seems to be in order in your report. It will—as it should—remain locked and classified for our eyes only. But I have a question. Did you notice the one thing both the Progons and Sensaurians did in answer to my message? They had wildly different approaches to my message, but did you notice that one similar thing?"

Ambassador X thought for a moment. The two reactions couldn't be more different. But there was one similarity he could think of. "They wouldn't acknowledge the Dimensional War," he answered.

The Secretary snapped. "Exactly! The Sensaurians didn't deny it. They pretended like they didn't know what you were talking about. The Progons just didn't react at all. Typical Progon maneuver. You wouldn't know this, but they can be very talkative and even nosy when they want. They are individuals. But they held you at more than arm's length. Why?"

"I don't know. Why?"

"I don't know either." The Secretary giggled. "And that's what's so valuable about your report. We now have a piece of information we didn't have. Both sides—the emotional, personality-driven machine race and the vast, clinical hive mind—feel it's in their best interests to give nothing away about what they know or think of the Dimensional War. That will tell me something later. It's a piece of the puzzle and an extremely valuable one."

The Secretary moved out from behind the desk. Ambassador X stood. The Secretary reached out and touched him on the shoulder. "Thank you, *Ambassador* X. Verity has your next assignment."

Ambassador X nodded, then left.

Outside the door was a Messenger. Ambassador X recognized him.

"Instructor X?" the Messenger asked.

"Still too early. Ambassador, I'm afraid."

The Messenger looked upset and stared down at his instructions. "They swore these were the right coordinates. Apologies, Ambassador X." And then he was gone again.

Back at the *Verity*, he asked about his assignment.

"The details were sent to me shortly after you departed. You are to proceed to Velkin 6 for postwar renormalization discussions."

"The Pineapple Planet?"

"There are very few pineapples on Velkin 6," stated Verity.

"I know. That's the joke. You're supposed to say, 'There are no pineapples there.' I thought you were getting a sense of humor."

"Yes, you did."

"Did what?"

"You did think I was getting a sense of humor."

"See?! I knew it. OK, who am I meeting with?"

"The President Pro Tem is Garrolan Four. He was the Secretary of Interior but is the highest-ranking member of the government left alive after the war."

"Looking over it now. Progons, Sensaurians, *and* us, all battling to keep each other away from that planet. It does have a rich biosphere, after all. Did. We almost wiped it out. But it looks like we drove everyone else off. Yay. We win." He did not sound in the least bit triumphant. "Where are we meeting? It says here the government buildings are all destroyed."

"We are to meet President Four in the Zooarium. It's how he survived the war. He was in charge of the department that preserves biodiversity. The Zooarium was never targeted for that reason."

"Wow. I'm getting this. Sensaurians moved in to try to add the biodiversity to their hive mind. Progons objected and started a war. Alendans came in to broker peace, and both sides turned on us. We set down on the planet and everybody came after us, burning as they went, destroying the thing they were fighting over. Eventually, we outlasted them. No armistice. They all just left. Poor Pineapple Planet. I'll dive into the checklist later, but what's the top line on the mission?"

"Your mission is to offer aid in postwar renormalization and the assistance of an Economist to begin beneficiary trade talks. Perhaps you could offer to solve their pineapple trade deficit as a start?"

Ambassador X wagged his finger. "Good try. You're getting better."

THE PINEAPPLE
PLANET

Velkin 6 had once been among the most beautiful planets in existence. Anything could grow there. At one point in its history, the planet's populace boasted they could grow even the most exotic offworld fruit. Someone had brought them an odd thing called a pineapple. It was a fruit that for some reason could not be made to grow anywhere but on its home planet, which was a sparsely populated water world of some sort.

The Velkin botanists took to the task and made it work. They were able to keep two pineapple plants alive consistently. Not always the same two but always two. Velkin 6 became known as the planet that could even grow a pineapple. That got shortened to Pineapple Planet eventually. Then, as these things go, the origin of the name got lost and people began to joke about the fact that a place called the Pineapple Planet had only two pineapple plants. Or almost no pineapples. And eventually that saying became "the Pineapple Planet has no pineapples."

Velkin 6 resisted the derogatory nickname at first, but eventually gave in and embraced it, selling pineapple trinkets and souvenirs and the best imported pineapple in the universe, which was still a great rarity.

That was all in its earliest past.

Now the planet was desolate. Clouds of ash covered most of the once-green world. Ambassador X asked Verity to descend slowly so he could get a good view of the damage, yet there was little to see but clouds until they neared the ground.

The Zooarium was in a large farming city, surrounded by an even larger refugee camp. Alendan aidcraft, parked in large numbers around the perimeter, came from all eras. Paradox Prevention had a mess to deal with, but the size of the devastation was enough to warrant the trouble. Alenda was doing good work here. Ambassador X allowed himself to feel a little pride mixed in with his sadness and horror.

He set down a short walk from the Zooarium. The air looked clear but smelled burnt, like a building site that had exploded, caught on fire, and been doused by a chemical spray.

People sat in clumps of two or three along the streets, some holding signs asking for the whereabouts of certain people, or making requests to trade for certain items. They identified him as an Alendan official and ignored him. They weren't beggars or protestors. They were survivors, and they knew Alendans were giving what they could outside the city. And in any case, he carried nothing of use to them, not now.

Velkin guards outside the Zooarium stopped him. They were the first non-Alendan military he had seen. They stood beside a temporary sign declaring the building the temporary capitol of Velkin 6.

"State your business," a dejected officer said. Lines crossed the man's face, but the stress that caused them had gone and left him slack. His war was over; he wanted only to rest.

"Ambassador X here to see President Pro Tem Four."

The officer nodded. He didn't check any lists. There weren't that many visitors. He didn't look at ID. Ambassador X's face was his ID. He only nodded and sat back down to rest. The other officer opened the door for him.

Nobody told him where to go or escorted him to the President. This was barely a government anymore. The Alendans ran things now. He was expected to find his own way. And he would.

The halls were only lighted every few hundred feet by small eternalights. These were a Velkin invention that used ambient kinetic energy to charge a battery that lasted centuries. They might go out sometimes, but over time they would recharge and come back on. He saw several dark ones, but most were lighted. The gyrations of war had charged most of them quite well.

He followed signs to the administration offices of the Zooarium, assuming the President would make that his center of command. He was wrong. Nobody was there but a maintenance person who didn't speak any of the languages Ambassador X knew, including Velkin's top three. Ambassador X thanked him anyway and set off toward the main exhibits. He figured if he wandered around long enough, he'd find someone who spoke a language he knew.

Eventually, he found himself in a large room filled with huge black circular spheres held in suspension. The spheres moved randomly. They were surrounded by equally large industrial printing boxes that hummed loudly and fed printed matter into the spheres through great tubes.

Near the front of the room the spheres were two or three times Ambassador X's height. In the back were three gargantuan spheres more than ten times his height. And in between all kinds of other sizes hung in a bowl-like depression.

Ambassador X leaned against a railing in the entrance walk-way and examined the room. At the bottom of the well, an old man wearing a brown robe bent over one of the printing boxes.

"Excuse me, sir, I'm afraid I'm lost," Ambassador X yelled down to the man.

"I doubt it," the old man yelled back.

"Say again?"

"I said I doubt you're lost."

"Yes, I thought that's what you said."

The old man nodded and kept to his work.

Ambassador X waited.

After a while the old man seemed to finish his task. He let out a sigh that seemed to be a mix of exasperation and relief and stood up straight. For the first time he looked up at Ambassador X. "Well, come down from there so I don't have to shout."

Ambassador X found his way down to the bottom of the well. It took him some time to navigate through the giant, slowly moving spheres. They moved without any discernible pattern. Some rolled slowly in place while others jerked in different directions. Finally, he reached the old man.

"That's better," the man said as Ambassador X approached.

"Yes, well, I was hoping you could direct me—"

"You're here," the man sighed.

"Right, well, I suppose that's always true wherever I am. I can always say I'm here. Can't rightly say I'm there. Well, as a matter fact, that's not true. In fact, recently I could say I was both there and there at the same time I said I was here and still be telling the truth. But that's neither here nor there." The old man winced at this, but Ambassador X carried on. "Because I'll always be here, no matter whether I'm also there. Time travel. Holy hell on your logic."

"Have it your way. I'm Garrolan Four, Secretary of the Interior and President Pro Tem of Velkin 6." The man held both hands out wide to the side in a traditional Velkin greeting.

Ambassador X returned the greeting. "You were right."

"About what?" the man said, surprised.

"I'm not lost."

President Garrolan chuckled. "I knew you'd come around to my way of thinking eventually. I suppose we're meant to go to some official state meeting area or something, except I haven't got anything like that. Just a few offices and desks in the administrative area. We used to all work down here for the most part. Didn't see the need for extra rooms that would go to waste." The man's voice began to drift and fade. "That's all changed now."

"When you did need to spend time talking with someone, where did you go?" Ambassador X asked.

"Often with the goat," Garrolan answered.

"The goat."

"Over there." The man pointed at one of the gently rolling spheres nearby. "That one. She doesn't smell, unlike the males. I do wish we had a good smelly male for her, though. Poor thing. That may never happen. Shall we?"

"Oh!" Ambassador X said, finally remembering that they were in a Zooarium. "The goat's in that thing, is it?"

President Garrolan just looked at Ambassador X like one looks at a hopeless child. "Come," he finally said.

The sphere rotated on top of a short base with a rounded-out depression of sorts. Some kind of energy beam controlled the sphere's direction. President Garrolan opened a door in the base. It was dark inside with only two small eternalights to see by. A short set of stairs led to a complicated mechanism that turned out to be some kind of door in the side of the depression at the top of the base. You could hear the metallic squeaks of the sphere turning and grinding.

Garrolan worked the mechanism and opened a sliding panel. A bright light shone out from a green meadow under a beautiful blue sky. A goat wandered along in the distance.

"You go first. It's a little tricky the first time. Just wait until you think you can make a step without falling. Once you have both feet inside, it won't feel like it's moving. I'll catch up."

Ambassador X stepped past Garrolan and saw what the man meant. The ground moved and shifted inside the sphere. As the goat walked, the sphere turned and grass near the edges slid around to keep the plain even. The blue sky was some kind of light panel that lined the interior of the sphere. When grass panels moved, sky panels disappeared underneath. They seemed to adjust their brightness as they rotated up, though.

The goat stopped to chew some grass, and Ambassador X decided that was the best time to step out into the sphere. It was a magical shift in perception. Once he had both feet on the ground, he could have sworn he was standing in a flat meadow. The goat just seemed to be ahead of him a bit on a small rise. President Garrolan followed in after him.

"It's a clever piece of work, but we have to stay close to the goat," the President said. He strode past Ambassador X and took the goat's collar. Whatever Garrolan did made the goat act as if she were tethered.

"That'll keep Shelly in line. So. How do you want to do this, Ambassador X? Long speech? Hard-earned negotiations? Or should I just tell you what we need and then you tell me how much you can give us?"

"I like the last," said Ambassador X.

"I thought you might. I hate negotiations. I'd rather let you 'win' than suffer through them just to gain a pittance."

"I intend to give you everything you ask for, if I can," Ambassador X said with a tone of gentle correction.

"Fine. Make the war not happen. This Dimensional War. Make it stop. Make it disappear. Can you do that? Can you give me my planet back?" The President's eyes were steel gray and steady.

"No," Ambassador X admitted.

"Of course not. Well. Here I said I wouldn't negotiate, but I suppose I must. Since I can't get what I really want."

The conversation turned to needs for security and food and resources. It was a reasonable list of requests, and Ambassador X found that he could easily grant most of it. The few things he didn't have the authority to approve, he promised to fast-track.

"We're time travelers. We can take years to debate something and still have it fast-tracked. Will tomorrow be sufficient for all your requests?"

"Thank you," the man said, grateful but sad. "It will. I do wish you could grant my first request, but I know you can't. No one can. One of your generals told me about fixed points and time threads and the limited nature of reality alteration and all that. I'm an expert in animals, not physics. But I suppose I understood enough. Still . . . Well. You've been more than fair. Let's let Shelly go now, so she can enjoy herself."

He manipulated her collar again. The goat didn't seem to notice. She methodically cropped the grass.

President Garrolan looked around the sphere and sighed. "I've thought about making one of these for myself. Those printers out there keep the spheres filled with an endless supply of vegetation and air and all the things an animal needs. We try to keep them in natural situations. Packs for the pack animals, solitude for the loners. Families for those who need them. They hardly know they're in a cage. Survival rate and health is a mere fraction of a percentage point less than wild specimens. Or was. The wild specimens all died in the war. So I wonder if I'd be happier in here sometimes. But I guess I wouldn't be. Too curious. That's our problem."

Garrolan slid the door out. The sphere wasn't moving at the moment, so the two of them easily slipped out onto the staircase. The goat started to walk just as Ambassador X stepped off; he got vertigo for a second but recovered.

Outside among the spheres again, Ambassador X made the traditional Velkin wide-open gesture of respectful parting. "It has been an honor to meet you, President Garrolan Four."

"You too, Ambassador X."

"My only regret is not seeing a pineapple plant," Ambassador X deadpanned.

"There are no pineapples here," Garrolan said, frowning.

"I'm sorry."

"Take care, Ambassador X. Don't let one sad old man get you down. But . . ." He paused, uncertain of himself for the first time since Ambassador X had met him. "If you ever discover— if you ever find a way by some chance—to put it all right, I hope you will."

Ambassador X nodded. Garrolan Four turned away and walked back into the spheres, disappearing.

X

Ambassador X had no more meetings with the Secretary. He met with small civilizations just making their first steps onto the universal stage. He met with old civilizations just wanting to be left alone. Most often he met with devastation. A long-time enemy suddenly grew powerful and drove a civilization into exile. An unknown enemy appeared and waged war for no discernible reason. In all cases, Ambassador X was able to help the victims recover. But he could not help them understand. He didn't understand himself.

His most unexpected assignment came from the hermits.

The planet was known as the Hermitage for most of its inhabited history, though it had been uninhabited for a majority of its existence. It contained no significant natural resources. The climate was stark. It was only about thirty percent water, and most of that was salty ocean. The land was majority rock. The inhabitable areas were barely vegetated with few streams or wildlife.

A few mining colonies were attempted but went broke fast. Researchers and scientists visited, but their studies found little of any value and they moved on quickly. It finally became a refuge for hermits. They came from all species, except for the Sensaurians. There was even a Progon hermit. These loners preferred no contact with others. The Hermitage planet was perfect for that. Nobody but other hermits came there. There was just enough of a biosphere to scrape by.

The few things needed from offworld were provided by a single trading post. It had expanded into a full general store at one point with a market and even a few souvenirs for the extraordinarily rare visitor. However, the owner had started to get ideas about creating a tourist destination. When she tried to charter visits, the usually unflappable hermits got angry. It was the closest to starting an organized government the planet ever got. Several of the hermits gathered together and demanded the owner leave the planet.

After that, the store shrank back into a trading post, run by a series of people content with providing the few goods the hermits required with no ambitions beyond that. That's what made the assignment so odd for Ambassador X.

A hermit had requested Alendan assistance. She asked to meet Ambassador X at the trading post to give further

information. It was a voluntary assignment. The Alendans
had acknowledged the request but not committed to it. Since
Ambassador X did not have any conflicting mandatory assignments at the moment, he could not resist.

X

The *Verity* set down as close to the trading post main building
as it safely could. A quiet woman named Fer was the current
proprietor. She met Ambassador X at the door and offered him
food and drink, which he declined.

The trading post's main building was the only one in use. It
was a one-story wooden structure set apart from the ruins of
the others, surrounded by dusty ground. There were no windows, but the door hung open most of the time. Two hand-
built wooden chairs sat in the strip of shade under the awning
next to a small hand-built table.

Ambassador X asked if the hermit who had requested
assistance knew he had arrived, and Fer nodded. She showed
Ambassador X to one of the chairs and asked him to wait.
After a while, he went inside the trading post anyway. Shelves
lined the floors filled with practical goods like rope, salt, tools,
and the like. Fer sat behind a tiny table, not even a desk, read-
ing a book. She looked at Ambassador X disapprovingly but
said nothing.

He began to peruse through the shelves, curious what
kinds of things they stocked.

"You call it a trading post. What do the hermits trade?" he
asked.

Fer glared at him. "Things they find or make," she finally
said when she realized he would continue to wait for an answer.
"Rope. Some evaporate water for salt. Like that."

"So you don't use any kind of money?" he asked.

"No," she said and then added, "your visitor will be looking for you out front."

He took the hint. Outside, a young woman wearing a simple linen dress sat in one of the chairs.

"Ambassador X?" she asked, standing.

"Who else?" he shrugged. "And you are?"

"Trink. I'm the one who contacted you."

"So I gathered," Ambassador X answered. He didn't know the proper greeting for a hermit, so he made no gesture.

"Please sit," Trink said, sitting back down herself.

"So what can the Guardians of Alenda do for you?"

"Not much," she said. "But I'm more optimistic about what you can do."

"What do you mean?" he said.

"I reached out to Alenda because they send diplomats throughout the universe investigating and aiding war-torn societies," she said using an archaic word for civilizations. "Am I correct?"

"Yes. That is my job."

"Exactly what I'd hoped. I need to ask questions of someone who has seen the devastations happening throughout the universe. And am I correct that you travel in time?"

"That is correct." Ambassador X felt out of his depth. This hermit had command of him. She didn't seem to be certain about what he or his people did, and yet she knew much more than he expected. He was curious to hear her questions.

"Good. The historical perspective may be quite helpful. Ambassador X, hermits have been disappearing."

"I'm sorry to hear that. What do you think is the reason?"

"War," she said.

"The hermits are at war?"

"No, the war is hiding on Hermitage," she said. "But let me hold off explaining that. I have a few questions if I may."

Ambassador X's head spun. "Of course. Go ahead," he managed to say.

"Is there a vast war happening across time and hidden from most other civilizations?"

Trink was not one to pull a punch. "That is the question," Ambassador X said. "We suspect so."

"We?" she asked.

"The Alendans."

"If I were to guess, the Alendans as a whole have little knowledge. But the Alendans in charge are participating and keeping you mostly in the dark. Your answer tells me much. Next question. Have you been able to stop the war anywhere and bring relief instead?"

Ambassador X breathed a sigh of relief. "Yes, I have."

"Good." She nodded mostly to herself. "Final question. Can you help me the same way you've helped others?"

Ambassador X looked at her but could only see true sincerity.

"It's a question I cannot answer properly based on what you've told me alone. But I can say I will try."

"That will have to be good enough. I would like to show you some things near my home that may help you understand. Will you be my guest tonight?"

This definitely threw Ambassador X. He wouldn't have guessed hermits were set up for guests.

"I don't mean to be rude, but how would that work?"

Trink laughed. It was like breaking glass and a peal of bells. "You will see. But I can assure you if you're not looking for luxury, you'll be quite comfortable."

X

The light faded as they walked through the scrubby land to Trink's home. She lived not far from the trading post in a squat shack made of local brush. The building was divided into three rooms.

One of the rooms had a bed and washing area for Ambassador X. There was even a small space that worked as a shower and cleaning sink.

"Do you have guests often?" Ambassador X asked.

"No. I created this especially for you," she said. "Or not you personally, but whomever the Alendans sent."

"It must have been costly," he said.

"I'd saved." She laughed. "I hadn't had much else to spend it on. Only so much rope and salt I need, you know? I'll leave you to it."

Normally, Ambassador X would have declined to stay. The *Verity* was much more comfortable. But he wanted to know more about Trink, and he wanted to get an early start.

The next morning, Trink made Ambassador X some kind of hot oatcake and a hot black beverage that wasn't coffee but certainly was meant to appear and taste close to it. It didn't, but he appreciated the gesture.

The oatcake was satisfying if unremarkable. It was a feast next to what Trink ate. She spooned thin gruel from a pottery bowl.

Ambassador X recognized it. "Is that emergency protein-ration soup?" he asked.

She smiled. "Cost-effective and easy to prepare. Lets me focus on other things." He started to ask her something else, but she interrupted. "Have you ever been to this point before?"

She meant Hermitage, but her phrasing caught his attention. "Point?"

She laughed again. She laughed a lot for a hermit. "Giveaway, isn't it, saying point instead of place?" she said with a mischievous look.

"You're Alendan!" he almost shouted.

She nodded. "Yes. But not a time traveler like you. I was once part of the Alendan Core. For a while."

"I was supposed to meet with them once. They never showed up. Or if they did, they didn't let me know who they were. You're the first person I've met who admitted to being part of them."

"They're not really as mysterious as people think. But they know the rest of Alendan society misunderstands them, so they try not to call attention to themselves. It's actually a very supportive community. It's not a cult. They'll let you leave anytime, but most people don't want to. Most people who make their way into the Core find fulfillment there."

"So why did you leave?" he asked.

"I spent a long time looking for truths. I traveled, just not in time. Many colleagues and friends said I should leave the Core and time-travel to find the answers I sought. But I didn't. I know history. The answers aren't there, or in the future either, I suspect."

"And you think they're here?"

"I think they're here," she said pointing at her head. "Coming here has let me focus. I've learned so much more, sitting and contemplating, than I ever did being distracted and confused all the time."

Ambassador X laughed this time. "I couldn't do it. I'd die for companionship."

"Maybe you would," she said, gathering up the dishes. "You're not meant for solo life. But I think you're still not a crowd person. You haven't once complained of the lack of people or amenities. In fact—" She paused. "I'd guess your ship is all you need. Am I right?" She turned to put the dishes in a tub for cleaning.

"It's a small truth, but I think you found one."

She laughed again. "I've found a few that are a little bigger. But I have some facts that need another person to deal with. I'm not a zealot. I know when I need help. Come, let's go. An example of what I mean is not far from here."

X

They walked most of the morning. Everywhere Ambassador X went on Hermitage looked pretty much the same. There were no mountains. No real hills. Just rolling plains and scrubby vegetation with small rivulets hardly worth calling streams.

He saw where they must be headed long before they got there. It was a change in the landscape, black and charred. Something had burned or crashed. They walked in silence until they arrived.

A huge depression in the land had been created by several wrecked pieces of battleships. A war had been fought in the space above, and its shrapnel landed here. It would not be an odd scene if it were on Velkin 6. But it was like seeing a wolf in a clothing store on Hermitage.

"When did this happen?"

"Right before I sent the message. It's what shook me into contacting Alenda. You came to a point soon after I sent it, so maybe five or six days ago local time?"

"But we have no record of a battle here. These are Progon parts, and those look like Sensaurian bucket pilot pods—"

"And that is an Alendan fighter cockpit," she said.

"You're right," he admitted.

"You must have heard or seen the battle for this to fall here."

She shook her head. "I only heard the impact. I spoke with other hermits nearby. They say the same. The skies were peaceful. Many of them contemplate it regularly, so many eyes were on the heavens. There was no battle. Only the fallout of one."

"What an odd occurrence," Ambassador X mused.

"If only it were so," she countered. "After you leave me, you can orbit to confirm this, but there are dozens in this area alone. This is the first one to happen this close to me, but they've happened all over. Fer could tell you how many. The hermits who do talk, talk to her."

"You're telling me that wreckage from battles is falling out of the sky regularly on Hermitage, but no battles are taking place above?"

"Correct," she said.

"I just don't understand."

"But you can. I can't. This is something I can't discover by thinking about it."

"I suppose not."

"Can you help me the same way you've helped others?" she repeated her question from the day before.

After a long pause, he said, "I can."

"Will you?" she probed.

"I must."

Then suddenly she put her hand on his shoulder and pulled his gaze away from the wreckage toward her. Her eyes fluttered up into her head. "I have thought long on this," she said in a monotone. "The threads must be undone. This rope is long but frayed and wrong. Only one can make the instant right. Only one can break dawn on this long night. Be bold, X. Be brave, X. Be strong, X. What you will do is right."

She lowered her arm, and her expression returned to normal. She smiled. "My apologies. Those inspirations come on me and I've learned to trust them." She shrugged. "I hope it proves useful in some way. If not, well, you can quote it at parties." She laughed. "Hermit verse."

"What *was* that?" he said slowly.

"That was the product of my focus and thinking out here."

"All right, Trink. I'll try to remember what you said. Do you even know what you said?" He realized maybe she didn't.

She repeated it verbatim and a little self-consciously.

"It's kind of overdramatic and a bad rhyming scheme," she admitted. "But they usually have insight all the same. I'm a hermit, not a poet."

They walked back to Trink's home and collected the few things he had left there, then she showed him the way back to the trading post. They never saw another person, but then that was the point of Hermitage. Fer answered a few of his questions about the reports of wreckage from other hermits. She didn't volunteer much and seemed relieved when he was done talking to her. Trink walked him to his ship.

"For a hermit you're awfully friendly," he said. "I thought you'd scamper back up to your ho—home as soon as you could."

"You were going to say 'hovel,' weren't you? It's OK. I'm a hermit, yes. I enjoy being alone and thinking. But it doesn't mean I fear others. Not like Fer. She's here because she fears others but doesn't want to be alone. Perfect job for her. Constant visits from people who want to be alone. She found her niche. But don't worry. I also found mine. I think you are on your way to finding yours too, Ambassador X."

"Oh, I found mine. This is what I love."

She cocked her head at this. "Not yet. But very close. Take care, Ambassador X." She touched his shoulder and turned to begin the walk back to her home.

Inside, Verity took his report and plotted a surveillance orbit of Hermitage. They found hundreds of crash sites. Given the number of sites, there should have been tons of debris in orbit too, but orbital space was clean.

"What could cause battle wreckage to appear suddenly above a planet and fall to the ground without a battle ever occurring anywhere near the planet?" he asked aloud.

"A singularity," Verity answered.

"Verity, you're a genius," Ambassador X said.

THE MISSION

Upon his return to Alenda, Ambassador X gave his report to Ambassador Le. The Assistant to the Secretary had been made a full Ambassador, but she still served under the Secretary.

"You can tell me everything," she said to Ambassador X. He felt fairly certain this was a slight jab at the fact that he had refused to give her his report back when he was a Pilot. But this time, he held nothing back. He had no reason to. He wasn't feeling spiteful.

"So you made one personal ground inspection and several orbital inspections?" she asked without looking up while taking notes.

"Yes."

"Have you submitted visual records?"

"No."

"Why not?" Her tone suggested there could be numerous reasonable excuses for not following procedure. There were.

"The nature of the records was such that uninformed interpretation could lead to incorrect and damaging conclusions, especially among the populace at large," he quoted.

"Section 7.06?" she summarized.

"Just so."

She looked up from her notes. "It's OK to quote rules and regs by number with me," she remarked, then looked back down. "What is your confidence level that these ruins were valid?"

He hadn't estimated that. "Pretty confident." He smiled.

"So you don't have Kourou Scale value assigned?"

"How about 'high'?" he joked.

She didn't seem to appreciate the joke. "I'll write seventy-five percent unless you object."

"I'd say ninety," he interrupted before she could note it.

"And you have the Kourou Scale work to back that figure up?" He sensed the slightest twitch to the corner of her mouth. Ah-ha. This was what made a joke to her.

"I haven't claimed otherwise. Say ninety-two percent."

She nodded.

"Will the visual records show Progon, Sensaurian, and Alendan markings clearly, or will your logs be needed to bolster authenticity?"

He hadn't thought of this either.

"I'd have to ask Verity," he said. "But my logs will bolster it."

She sent a request to the *Verity*.

"My ship has you on its communications list?" he asked.

"She requested it." The twitch again.

"Oh. Well. Machines will talk."

Her head jerked up.

"I mean Verity, of course," he answered, grinning again.

This time she broke into a cold smile. The kind of smile you give to a worthy opponent. No love. Just admiration for the move.

"This is very concerning. Your 7.06 protection is correct and definitely necessary. This is Secretary's eyes only from here on."

Ambassador X went back to the *Verity* to relax and wait for his next assignment. He asked Verity about Ambassador Le.

"When I received the information she had been made a full Ambassador, I contacted her and made communication available. I anticipated her reputation for meticulous records might require it someday."

"You always think ahead, Verity."

"Water is wet," the ship responded.

"Your sense of humor is coming along quite well."

"Was that funny?" she asked.

"See?!"

"The Secretary has sent a private request for a meeting in his office," Verity said.

"Still joking?"

"I am not joking."

"He didn't say which office?" It wasn't like Verity not to be precise when passing along information.

"The message lists the Secretary's main office as the location."

"Oh! His real office."

"It would seem so."

"Well, this will be interesting."

"Ready to depart," Verity answered.

X

It was still a dirty planet, young and unorganized. Its inhabitants would not be civilized or respectable neighbors for centuries more after that. Eventually, though, they would become the most respected species in existence. Ambassador X knew this because he was one of them.

The Secretary made his office in this space-time point because of this juxtaposition. Anyone arriving saw the planet in its ancient state. He felt the Guardians of Alenda should never forget their heritage.

Unlike Ambassador X's previous visit to this era, this particular arrival point was unfixed. The conditions were such that nothing visitors could do would affect any significant events. Butterflies flapped their wings in vain here. The outside winds were too strong.

Ambassador X landed the *Verity* a short walk from the rough mud hut the Secretary called his real office. He resolved to be cooperative this time and hopefully put things with the Secretary back on an even keel.

When Ambassador X arrived at the hut, he found fifty people from various species lined up in parade formation outside. The Secretary stood in front drilling them on something. It was hard to tell what. He barked unintelligible words, and the people responded in their own languages.

A pink octopod in shiny silver laser armor stood next to a Lemring monopod attached to a wheeled motivator. Next to them was a strange-looking fishlike creature Ambassador X couldn't place, who seemed to be riding in a Sensaurian bucket and wearing a breathing mask. A biped species wearing brown cloth with flat hair and a bushy dash of a mustache on an otherwise hairless face stood next. That one was dwarfed by a gigantic red scaly creature wrapped in what would have otherwise been a pretty green sari.

Agent Asa was nowhere to be seen.

"Private army?" Ambassador X inquired as he came into earshot.

The Secretary snapped his head toward Ambassador X and grinned. "Special assignments! These fine leaders are being trained to take control of their civilizations in support of the Alendans. Some of them have tall tasks, including the unification of their worlds. But they all are masters now. We're about to send them off to their various planets. I call them the Manic Masters!"

"That may not sound as good out loud as it does in your head," Ambassador X mused.

The Secretary waved him off. "Dismissed!" he shouted to the group, and they moved off into the forest.

"Glad you got to see them, though," the Secretary said as he motioned Ambassador X toward the mud hut. "They're a key to the Dimensional War. I intend to litter these crack leaders throughout space-time like mines. When the Progons or Sensaurians try to take their planets, they'll snap like a trap!"

"Fantastic," Ambassador X said, following the Secretary into the hut.

It was a little larger than Ambassador X remembered, though the interior was still rough. The Secretary hadn't done much to spruce it up over the years. He easily could have constructed a modern technological space hidden from the natives. Instead, he lived, dressed, and smelled period-appropriate.

"Have a seat. Apologies as usual for the lack of comforts, but—well, you know the reasons." The Secretary looked abashed.

Ambassador X had learned the reasons repetitively. The Secretary wanted as little pollution of the planet as possible. Not because of effects on the timeline, but the Secretary's own ecological sensitivities. He just didn't like the idea of the planet all mucked up before Alendans even discovered the steam engine. He also liked to feel the discomfort of his visitors. Ambassador X remembered that all too well.

"I've asked you here because it's time for you to take another difficult journey, the end of which even I can't see. This journey is the reason I've had to be so hard on you sometimes. It's the reason you were trained and became an Ambassador. It will be the hardest test you've ever faced, and as bad as I feel for what you've gone through, you could not face this next journey without having done so."

This was not the usual opener.

"The Progons and the Sensaurians are on the move. Both in different eras. The effects are spread out over a vast amount of space and time."

"You think we would have noticed that before," Ambassador X ventured.

The Secretary nodded. "A few of us have. Certainly. But only in the corners. It's like that old philosopher's story about our home planet. If an alien landed blindfolded in the Jerendran Desert and took off his blindfold, he'd think he landed on a desert planet. If he landed in a forest, he'd think he landed on a forest planet, et cetera. We travel all through space and time, but we still only see a corner of it."

"So what's this issue, then?"

"The Dimensional War. It's time you learned more about it. Your observations on Hermitage have probably led you to guess a lot of this. Hermitage is sort of the end of an exhaust pipe for the huge machinations that keep the war hidden. It's the greatest war that ever existed. And yet the greatest secret ever kept. Some of our own have turned against us and threaten to undermine us from within or without. We have to be extremely careful who we trust. Our enemies, even some Alendans, mean to end the Guardians' protection of the universe and change every unfixed point.

"Ambassador X." He stood. "It's a war only you can prevent or end. I'm sorry."

The Secretary was not joking. He used Ambassador X's correct title. For the first time in their relationship, the Secretary seemed to be dealing straight. Ambassador X bowed his head. Any remaining annoyance with the Secretary fled.

"What do I do?"

"You start with another mission of peace. A real mission of peace, not a gesture. A much greater demonstration than before. This time you will not just be a messenger. First I'm sending you to the Progons. After that to the Sensaurians. This time you won't ask. You must rearrange their motivations in such a way to limit the war to a more conventional size and save the universe."

"And if I fail? Do I fail?"

"Even I don't know if you do. It's that obscured. But if you do, you'll have another option. A horrible one, but an option nonetheless. You'll learn it in time."

Ambassador X got up to leave.

"Oh, one more thing," the Secretary said. "Two more, actually. Hold on to the *Verity* tightly. You're a Pilot at heart. Don't forget that."

Ambassador X nodded. "And the other?"

"Don't trust the Vice Counsel's plan. That's all I can say. All I need say, I think. Good luck, Ambassador X."

Luck. It was a word the Secretary never used. It was frightening that he did so now.

X

Before Ambassador X was even through the door, Verity had plotted coordinates to the Progon homeworld of Tiel.

"The assignment came in as you were speaking with the Secretary," she said.

"From where?"

"From Agent Asa."

"I didn't see her there."

"She wasn't. She stopped by here and delivered them personally."

"Don't tell me you have her on your contact list too?"

"No. But she had emergency protocols. I could not deny her access. She left you a message."

"Oh?"

"She said to tell you 'thanks for the ride.' She said you'd know what it meant soon."

"Lovely. Anything else?"

"She delivered these supplementary mission instructions."

A briefing on both the Progon and Sensaurian assignments was included. He was to proceed to Tiel and take residence as a diplomat. He was being assigned to a sensitive time point after a thousand-year peace. The previous Ambassador hadn't lasted long and was now in the hospital. He'd have to read more about that later.

His main assignment was to not go insane but to lead the Progons to think he was. Progons of this era isolated diplomats and wore them down until they were dying to leave. They would either crack and provide Progons with valuable intelligence or rush negotiations in order to have an excuse to leave for their homeworld.

Ambassador X was chosen because of his mental stability shown in the secret training session with the Secretary. He needed to outlast the Progons at their own game, then sue for lasting peace.

"Well," he sighed. "Time to go play chess with the machines."

"Departing to Tiel now."

MISSION TO TIEL

Tiel appeared to be on fire. That was normal. On many planets, vegetation blended together to make land appear green. On Tiel, individual fires blended together to make land appear orange. Gas fields and generators burned across much of Tiel in a massive conflagration. They powered the great machines in which the Progons lived.

This was one of the many reasons Alendans worked hard never to get assigned to Tiel. There were few places on the planet that weren't deadly to Alendans, and fewer people to spend your time with in the nondeadly sections. Not to mention the Progons were sworn enemies of Alenda throughout most of time and space.

Ambassador X had been assigned as a diplomat in a relatively calm stretch, in order to get the Progons in a more cooperative era. He was only the second Alendan to serve as diplomat in more than a thousand years at this point. The first had lasted a week before having to be committed. Ambassador X was fairly certain it was a faked mental illness. And he thoroughly understood.

It was all the same to the Progons. The individual water sacks called Alendans barely registered to a race made of electricity. If a single Alendan ever physically assaulted a Progon, it might break a circuit and electrocute the Alendan in the process. Also, Progons could use their timecoms to communicate through time, so they knew what happened and would happen at least as much as the time-traveling Alendans did. In fact, they knew some things much quicker because they only had to ask their far-flung machines what was going on. Alendans had to travel in space as well as time.

That didn't mean there weren't gaps in their knowledge. No race could be at all points in space-time. So there were always mysteries. And this stretch of Progon time was a mystery to the Alendans. To be fair, this stretch of Alendan history was also unknown to the Progons. They had carefully arranged to stay out of each other's way for one thousand years. Ambassador X did not love the idea of disturbing that quiet period. For one, the Progons could call ahead to their future selves and find out what he did before he knew he would do it. He hated that about them. For another it meant he was the one to break the fragile peace that led to the greatest war in history. A war that Alendan High Command now knew raged in all manner of previously unknown stretches of history.

It had happened, was happening, and would happen in many regions of space-time. Ambassador X's mission was to mitigate it and find out why it happened at all.

Ambassador X's only protection was the *Verity*. Within it, the Progons could not see him. The *Verity*'s encapsulated singularity gave him a vast ship's interior, lush with rooms, swimming pools, theaters, and anything else one could think of. It also existed outside of normal space-time, giving him a shield against attempts to see the parts of his future or past that existed within the influence of the singularity.

It was the only way he could do this job.

He floated around Tiel for two more orbits before finally answering the relentless, mindless request for identification from the Tiel capital.

"Ambassador X of Alenda requesting diplomatic courtesies and permission to land in the capital."

"Permission granted," the voice spoke through static. It wasn't a Progon. It was just a machine. Ambassador X might never interact with an actual Progon during his entire time on the planet. The machines were why the Progons were thought of as a race of robots. The Progons themselves were much more insidious than robots. They had feelings and art and culture of a sort. But each individual was an electrical circuit. Their beliefs were so alien it was almost impossible for a waterbag like Ambassador X to grasp them. That alone wouldn't have been so bad if the Progons were not also convinced that they alone had a pure and dominant culture and all other beings should be subservient, like their machines.

"If only the robots really did rise up against their masters, ever," mused Ambassador X. Then he took the *Verity* out of orbit and headed down to the surface to begin his mission.

EMBASSY

The *Verity* descended toward a stretch of identical, evenly spaced one-story metal buildings. The Progons famously built down not up, so buildings generally looked alike from the air. Building down led them to more efficient material conversion or some such thing. The Progons were always about efficiency. Ambassador X's approved approach vector led him to one particular building that slowly opened to reveal a hangar. Besides the standard spaceport landing equipment, the hangar was empty except for a lone figure.

The *Verity* touched down, and before Ambassador X could finish a landing checklist, a warning bell sounded. "External lockdown applied, all systems suspended," the ship told him. Not surprising, but disconcerting. It was the space-travel equivalent of spooky castle doors shutting behind you and locking.

The Progons sent a bipedal robot to meet him. That was an unusual sign of deference. Progon machines came in all kinds of form factors, but few were bipedal. It wasn't a necessary form for almost anything they did. The Progons generally didn't care about making visitors feel at home either, so it felt like they were trying to flatter him.

"Ambassador X, welcome to Tiel," said the robot. It was likely an automaton, not an inhabited machine, but Ambassador X wondered. The Progons preferred to stay in large structures, communing with each other in their electron-fast existence, rather than dealing with the slowness of machines and the tedium of speaking aloud like an animal.

Progons could inhabit their robots and automata whenever they wanted, and it was difficult to tell when they did. A Progon was undetectable without an oscilloscope. Beings of pure electricity could only move through conducting materials but could do that almost invisibly. You could theoretically have a conversation with a machine on Progon and, in the course of the conversation, talk to the robot mind as well as several different individual Progons, and you'd never know.

Although Progons claimed they never did this and preferred to let their robots be robots.

"Thank you," Ambassador X ventured to the automaton/possible-but-unlikely Progon. "What may I call you?"

"Assistant," said the robot in a not unpleasant tone. Progons. They had names. Their robots had names. But they just sucked at translation. "Assistant, er, 5." The robot seemed to make it up on the spot. "If you'll follow me, I'll show you to your quarters."

They left the hangar by a metal walkway that led directly to other square metal buildings. The Progons did like their right angles. Here and there in the distance, other automata went about their business, but Ambassador X didn't see another soul. Of course the Progons could have flitted into and out of the robot and even the buildings around him without his ever knowing.

There were other Ambassadors from other civilizations on the planet as well. Some four hundred and fifty-three thousand of them. Each one was kept apart from the others, equally spaced across the planet, to prevent them from composing a threat or hatching a conspiracy.

It was a type of psychological warfare. Ambassadors on Tiel did not commune with their own kind and only had automata to speak with. It drove some mad. The previous Ambassador hadn't gone mad, just requested an urgent transfer for "family reasons." At least that's what the Alendans told the Progons.

The robot opened a sliding door at the end of one gangway and motioned Ambassador X to enter. Inside was what appeared to be a one-story flat. If there were lower stories, there was no obvious way of entering them. The quarters were sufficient. On the left was a circular mat that likely served as a bed. Ambassador X knew it was meant to serve a multitude of species, hence the shape and odd texture.

On the right was a small table that served as a desk and eating area with a chair and a few outlets for connectivity and such. Along the back wall was the kitchen. Large cabinets were set in the wall next to a mounted food-preparation machine. A sink of sorts, at least something that looked like it, dispensed water. A lower wide bowl was set off on its own with a closable divider, meant for bathing or possibly excretion or, knowing the Progons, both.

The robot opened the cabinets to reveal stacks of identical bars wrapped in white paper. One side of the cabinet was refrigerated.

"We have provided Alendan foods for your preparation. Stocks will be replenished automatically. Should you require other foods, please make your request through the diplomatic channel you were assigned."

In other words, you can fill out some paperwork, but don't expect anything but these bars. The robot moved to the sliding door.

"These buttons control the door. If you need to leave, please alert us to your planned movements through your assigned diplomatic channel. You are expected out for exercise between the fourth and sixth hours."

In other words, except for your daily jog, don't leave unless we tell you to. There really wasn't any need to. A diplomat's life on Tiel consisted of relaxation, exercise, regular diplomatic meetings with a Progon representative (usually an automaton), and wide stretches of boredom.

"May I be of assistance in any other matters, Ambassador X?" the robot asked.

"No, thank you Assistant, er, 5," Ambassador X mimicked the robot's delivery. "You've been efficient."

It was meant as flattery, but the robot showed no visible reaction.

"If you have further needs not previously covered by me—" *Submit them through your assigned diplomatic channel,* Ambassador X finished for the robot in his head. But instead it said, "Use the communicator button on the provided device and call for Assistant 5. Have a pleasant day, Ambassador X."

The robot left through the sliding door. What was that about? A last-minute parting shot of flattery? A communication device. Why hadn't the robot pointed it out? Ambassador X looked around the spacious if sparse room. He saw no communication device. Was it a trick? A taunt? Then he saw it. Lying on the edge of the circular bed near the wall.

It was a small, flat metal box with three buttons, one of them marked *Comm* in Alendan.

Ambassador X had the impulse to call the robot back immediately just to see if it worked. But he didn't. Still, this was not standard procedure as far as he knew. The departing Alendan Ambassador's brief made it clear that he had no way of communicating directly to the Progons, probably to increase his isolation. Ambassador X didn't want this unexpected perk to be taken away due to misuse.

So what did the other buttons do? One white button was labeled *Lights*. He pressed it and the lights in the room dimmed. Another modern convenience. Other Ambassadors reported the lights staying on at all times, messing with sleep patterns. The last green button was unlabeled. He pressed it but nothing happened. At least nothing he could tell. Maybe it blew up his ship in the hangar. Maybe it turned off the lights in some Progon room halfway across the planet.

He shrugged and tossed the device on the bed. Suddenly, the door ripped open and two rolling boxes with surgical arms came rushing in and grabbed him.

"What is the nature of your emergency?" they shrieked.

"Whoa, whoa! No emergency! I didn't report an emergency!"

"You pressed the green emergency button. The green emergency button is meant to indicate an emergency."

"A unlabeled green button is your emergency button?" Ambassador X chuckled. "Bad design, Progons."

TIME ON TIEL

In some ways Ambassador X felt like he was reliving his time with the Secretary on old Alenda. He wasn't building a mud hut and there was only one of him, but he was lonely and totally separated from Verity.

Most Pilots were attached to their ship, of course, but Verity was something special. She was evolving. He never mentioned it and rarely let himself think it. Artificial intelligences that showed signs of growth and evolution were quickly wiped. It was a serious crime not to report it. But it also needed to be evident. And if he didn't let himself think of it, he couldn't see it. And if he couldn't see it, it couldn't be reported.

But his jokes about a sense of humor were more than jokes. She was becoming a person. "The *Verity*" was a ship, but Verity was the person growing within her. Like an artificial womb. It made sense that he'd let himself think of this while on a planet filled with machines. He convinced himself to demand to see Verity as a way to convince them he was finally losing it. He wasn't, though. He was almost certain.

The robot announced itself at the door. Ambassador X got up to let it in.

"Assistant-er-5, so good to see you."

"I have come to see if there is anything I can do for you today?" It did this every day.

"Yes. There is." Ambassador X followed the usual script.

"What is it?" Assistant 5 asked. It had to know the answer by now.

"I would like to see Verity," Ambassador X said.

"Are you planning to depart?" Assistant 5 kept a straight face. Well, to be fair, the robot always had a straight face. It wasn't built to show expressions. Some robots were. Not Assistant 5.

"No, I just want to see the ship."

"I'm afraid that is not possible today. Your ship is secured in a hangar far from here. It would be a considerable effort to show it to you for no other purpose. Are you concerned about its safety?"

Ambassador X had learned early this was a trick question. If he insisted on expressing concern, it would be taken as a diplomatic incident. He would be allowed to see Verity in that case, but only as a prelude to his deportment back to Alenda. And he wasn't ready for that.

"No. I'm not concerned," Ambassador X said.

"That's good." Ambassador X actually thought he heard relief in the robot's voice.

"Is there anything else?" Assistant 5 turned a little as if to go. Ha! Anticipatory gesture. So it was a little bit aware of the repetitiveness of their conversations.

"Yes, there is," Ambassador X said.

The robot turned back sharply into an attentive posture. "What is it?"

"Do you know how to play chess?"

"No."

"Would you let me teach you? I'd like someone to play against."

"Yes."

"Excellent!"

Assistant 5 came in and sat down.

DEPARTURE
FROM TIEL

Ambassador X narrowed his eyes at the chessboard. Assistant 5 had played well and would likely checkmate within a dozen moves or so. The Progons, or their automata, had never played chess but learned it quickly. Neither one of those things was a surprise. Ambassador X had asked to play in order to figure out who, if anyone, controlled the robot. The style of play shifted just enough, especially in the early moves, that he was fairly certain the robot was occasionally inhabited by a Progon, maybe two different ones.

Progons almost never inhabited machines in front of non-Progons, and when they did, they occupied massive ceremonial machines designed to intimidate and ensure their security. The idea that they would build a humanoid machine and then inhabit it to spy on Ambassador X was extraordinary.

He stopped staring and made himself request permission to go for a walk. He'd been forcing himself to go for more walks. It was important for him to make sure the Progons did

not suspect any of his suspicions. Plus, he could show off his
pretended instability more outside. He felt like more eyes saw
him. Or sensors. Or whatever Progons used to observe him.
He was almost certain of it.

That's why he walked. At least that's what he told himself.
He wanted to seem like a typical diplomat going a little insane
in the enforced isolation.

Ambassador X was supposedly resistant to this and thus
would be able to discover the Progons' part in the secret war.
The Progons unexpectedly provided him more familiarity and
entertainment than any other diplomat he had ever heard of.
So he decided to push it. That's how he would force their hand.
He would act like he was succumbing to the pressures of isolation anyway. He would wander off his allowed walk and, if
confronted, rant about needing to see something new. The act
seemed very easy to pull off. Once he was ranting, they would
let their guard down and divulge useful information by accident. He was certain of it.

The surface of Tiel was an endless march of square metal
buildings. His plan was to get lost. That was easy enough.
Enforcer drones would fly to intercept him if he did, but they
would not harm him. The Progons respected diplomatic
immunity at least that much. They would only use force if he
tried to do something damaging or threatening. Wandering off
the prescribed path was against the rules but not cause for use
of force. It was, however, grounds for immediate expulsion. So
this better pay off.

Getting lost was just as easy as acting insane. He really was
lost. He could be two feet from his own metal box or several
clicks from it, he honestly had no idea. Well, he actually did
know because of the drones. They followed at a polite distance,
repeating their broadcast to turn around and return to quarters. That implied that he was headed away from his quarters.

So he trudged on, ranting aloud. Nothing sensible. Just whatever came to mind. A lot of it involved pie.

"Because you think you gave me such *amazing* food, but was there once pie? I mean any pie at all. Even freaking ratzenzen pie? No! And you know what else? Sky! You know," he screamed, "I need sky! You don't understand my needs. This place is a deathlake. A treason. Why did they put me here? Why did I agree?!"

The drones continued. "Ambassador X. Please calm down, turn around, and return to quarters. You are off the prescribed path and in violation of the terms of your acceptance."

A humanoid robot appeared from behind and began a new tactic, interrupting Ambassador X's ranting and placing a gentle metal hand on his shoulder.

"Please don't do this. We don't wish any ill toward you. We must do what is best."

The chess game had not only taught him when a different mind controlled the machine but also how that machine's communication changed. This one was controlled by a Progon now. It was uncharacteristically pleading.

Ambassador X stumbled on. As he reached another intersection, a change in the pattern occurred. A metal building blocked his path. He began to walk around it. The robot blocked him. The drones stopped their announcements.

"No," it said.

"Why?!" Ambassador X screamed, still in his ranting voice, but meaning it.

"We thought you would cooperate. We meant to bring some peace through you."

"Some?" This was it! They had divulged their secret. But their secret was they wanted peace? He was confused.

"We have deduced your mission. The war must happen. Must stay happened. It cannot be subverted. It must not.

But through you we can limit the damage. Prevent the total destruction your people would otherwise bring. That is your objective, no? Please stop."

Ambassador X knew the Secretary would never be satisfied with this. It was only words. He had to push them. He was certain of it.

The Progons were right. His objective was to get them to agree to limit the war. But not without knowing more about why they were waging it. So he walked around the building anyway. He could get more from them, he knew it.

Trees.

On the other side of the metal box were trees and a stream and green.

Ambassador X turned to look at the robot.

"What is this?"

"It would have been your home."

"My home?"

"After your mission. To save the universe."

"You presume so much."

"Because we know that you will end this. And we know you will decide if the Progons continue. We must continue."

The robot engaged a weapon.

"If I'm your only chance of salvation, you'd best not eliminate me."

"We cannot, but we must expel you. We will try again in an earlier time."

"Good luck with that," Ambassador X said. The *Verity* appeared above and landed. They must have released it from the hangar.

The Progon continued. "You have disappointed us greatly. But remember, for you we may have mercy. For the other Alendans, none."

"Worth remembering," said Ambassador X. Then he climbed in his small box of a ship and took off. He should return to the Secretary and report his partial success or, as the Secretary would see it, partial failure. But the Progons were not what the Secretary believed. Ambassador X knew they truly wanted to reach an agreement. And right then Ambassador X realized that the Secretary did not. He needed to know. Ambassador X reached a decision.

He fed space-time coordinates to Verity. The ship informed him it was a conjunction point. A coordinate in which events were locked and could not be experienced in alternate threads or have mainlines diverted.

"I'm counting on it," Ambassador X said. "Also tender my resignation with the Alendan Council. I'm going back to being a simple Pilot for a while."

Verity complied, submitting the request from Pilot X.

SENSAURIAN
AMBUSH

Pilot X returned near his home system about a day after he had originally left for Tiel and a day's travel from Alenda. His failure with the Progons was now several months in the future, and he wanted to prepare the Diplomatic Department for what was to come.

He was about to tell Verity to plot a course that would leisurely swing by the gas giants for some sightseeing when proximity alarms blared out of every speaker and the ship shuddered with a pounding from outside.

It sounded like rain.

"What is that?" he asked.

Verity displayed a visual of fine grains. There were no known debris fields this far out from the star. They were even outside his home system's Oort cloud. So what was that?

Verity zoomed in and analyzed. She determined the debris was made up of microcellular sentient pods of life.

"Sensaurians," he said aloud. It was the hive's annoying habit of pelting its targets with bits of itself before attacking. Exobiologists considered it a marking behavior meant to intimidate. Pilot X just considered it annoying. A Sensaurian battleship loomed into view off Verity's starboard bow and hailed him.

"So damned dramatic," muttered Pilot X. Then he answered the hail: "This is the Alenda ship *Verity* on a return diplomatic mission. Kindly stop raining pieces of yourself on my ship and let me go about my business."

The Sensaurians answered. "Ambassador X. We are aware of your business with the machine people. We have learned it from the future. We are aware of your meddling in our affairs as well. You cannot be allowed to continue. This path will lead to destruction for all. You must be killed for the greater good."

This was standard patter for the Sensaurians.

"Yes, yes. If you didn't always threaten to destroy every organism that wasn't you for the greater good, I might be flattered. And I'm not an Ambassador anymore, so I guess future you garbled the message. Perhaps it's best to let me finish what's left of my diplomatic mission while you get that sorted with your son."

"I am not my son. I am me forever," the Sensaurian battleship said pompously. "You must be destroyed not because of your threat to our mind, but because of your threat to all."

Well, that did seem to be a new twist. Sensaurians generally didn't care about anyone not Sensaurian. Also, they didn't work well with plurals other than *we* or *us*, so *all* was a heady and unusual concept for them.

"What do you mean by *all*?" Pilot X tried, hoping to confuse the Sensaurian with its own words.

"I cannot be confused by this. All is everything. And you will destroy everything if left on this timeline. We have seen it happen."

"You mean you will have seen it happen?" he countered.

"Yes. Tenses are malleable. Destruction imminent."

"Oh, stop. You'll start a war."

"No, you will. And this will stop it."

The battleship was charging a massive forward burst of fire targeted at the *Verity*.

"Verity, skip—" But the ship had already anticipated this and skipped forward one hour. Moving through such a small amount of space-time was tricky and difficult to do precisely. The hour turned out to be three days and closer to Alenda.

"Or that," said Pilot X. "Where's the battleship?"

Verity showed it on course to Sensaur. It had believed Pilot X destroyed.

"The bigger the hive mind, the dumber they fall." Pilot X chuckled. "Set course to—"

But Verity had already plotted a course to Alenda, swinging by the gas giants on the way.

"Well done, Verity. Well done."

AMBASSADOR X
RETURNS

"Did you hear Ambassador X arrived?"

"Yes, he flies himself, you know. So unusual. But then he has a timeship. He carries a singularity in his cabin. So it's a bit done for show, I should think."

"I heard he stepped down to become a Pilot again. Maybe that's why. But does his ship really have a singularity?"

"So I'm told, anyway. Timeships like that carry a whole pocket universe if the Pilots I've spoken with are to be believed. I've never flown in one."

"Seems dangerous, if you ask me."

"Well, perhaps that's why they don't."

"Don't what?"

"Ask you."

"Fair point."

"So is it true about the treaty?"

"If anyone can pull off a true peace with the Progons and Sensaurians, it's the Ambassador. Maybe that's why he quit. Can't top that."

"Only Bolger can go to Nollisar, eh?"

"Something like that. He's not like the other diplomats. Wasn't born into it."

"He's an Alendan though, no?"

"Oh yes, from the central planet and everything, but not one of the favored houses, if you catch my meaning. Not a house at all, really. Worked his way up. He's been at all sorts of jobs, Apprentice, Ambassador, of course Pilot, as you might expect."

"Would explain the small ship, I suppose."

"Explains the peace possibility too. Takes an outside perspective like his. That's what he's been doing the whole war. Racking that clever brain of his to find a solution."

"Have you met him before?"

"Once. He's a charmer, that's for sure. And a fast talker. It's no exaggeration that he can talk anyone into or out of doing pretty much anything. I knew he'd untie this knot we're in."

"So what happens to the, uh, conscripts, if you will?"

"I expect it will just be wound down now. Less said about all that the better. Ah, here he is. Ambassador X, a pleasure to meet you."

Pilot X, just stepping down from his ship, turned to greet the two men with a menacing smile.

"Ah, gentleman, you're just in time for some pinball." The two other men looked puzzled. "Be with you in an instant."

PEACE AT LAST

"Congratulations, Ambassador. We have a peace," the Secretary said.

Pilot X's resignation as Ambassador was official but not yet logged. So this time it was forgivable that the Secretary got the title wrong.

"I'm glad to hear that," Pilot X said. "How did that happen?"

The Secretary laughed. "You have gained an immense sense of humor. But modesty does not become you. Be proud. Only Bolger can go to Nollisar. Someday that will be 'only Ambassador X can go to Progon.'"

"I do so wish I was displaying my vast and depthless sense of humor, but in point of fact, I had to leave Progon ahead of schedule and I haven't taken my mission to Sensaur yet. Not the new one."

The Secretary nodded. "And you won't need to go on that mission. It's canceled. Look at this! I had assumed you'd seen it."

The Secretary showed Pilot X two messages. The first from the Progons started with the details of Ambassador X's departure but finished with a sworn promise. The known parameters of the

Dimensional War would not be expanded. The Progons would even provide a few details on Sensaurian-Progon conflicts.

The next message from the Sensaurians expressed their regret at the passing of Ambassador X, but as a gesture of their shock at his loss, they agreed to the outlines of limits to conflicts in multiple dimensions.

"So obviously we can't send you to negotiate the details. They think you're dead," the Secretary said. "Well, we could send a younger you, but you know we didn't. And they wouldn't accept that. It's not the way they do things. And we need a technical Ambassador for this anyway, not a field negotiator. This is a mop-up job. You did it! It was all worth it. I could not be more proud."

"So you're not curious why they think I'm dead?"

"I already found out. I asked you later. Brilliant, by the way."

"How so?"

"Stealing a robot from the Progons and having it assassinate you and throw you off the *Verity* in front of a Sensaurian diplomatic ship? Brilliant."

"Oh yes. That is brilliant." Pilot X wondered if he had just caused a paradox. He would now tell that story to the Secretary later. But he had just heard it from the Secretary. Unless. "Too bad it's not what happened."

The Secretary laughed and slapped himself in the head. "Paradox! So obvious. And you're so paradox-sensitive. But you used to bask so much in praise, you might not have noticed." The Secretary wagged his finger at Pilot X. "You've grown up on me!"

"So?" Pilot X probed.

"What?" the Secretary asked.

"Do you actually know why they think I'm dead?"

The Secretary actually looked embarrassed. "Well, you know I don't, since I just told that ridiculous story."

"Do you want to know? It's fine if you don't. I can keep a secret, you know."

"I'm on the edge. Of. My. Seat." The Secretary punctuated every word with a jerky movement as he walked over to a lounge seat in the temporary office.

"I told them."

"Told them what?" the Secretary smiled.

"Told them I was dead."

The Secretary shook his head. "I don't understand."

"They hailed me from their battleship near Alenda. I know you know that. There's no way that slips past the planetary Observers. So I told them Ambassador X was no more."

"And they bought it?"

"Yes. I offered a validated response. Truth-confimer. I said, 'I am not Ambassador X' and sent it to them. They independently confirmed it and were on their way."

The Secretary smiled with disbelief. "How did you pull that off? You couldn't have corrupted their own confirmation!"

"I was telling the truth."

"You were?"

"I'm Pilot X. I had already transmitted my resignation. Or—did you not get it?"

The Secretary giggled. "Well played. I hadn't. Well, that was brilliant." He slow-clapped in appreciation and stood. "You will be missed among the Ambassadors. And may I say, and I mean this, if you ever wish to return, say the word. I will reinstate you with no question. Especially after this."

Pilot X nodded his thanks.

"Now before we part, I want to offer you a new position. Something that will allow you to say 'I am not Pilot X' and be telling the truth."

"I'm intrigued," Pilot X said.

X

He left the Secretary's chambers satisfied that no one knew what really happened with the Sensaurians or the Progons. The Secretary would not therefore react in the way the Sensaurians and Progons planned, and the Dimensional War would not expand into the nooks and crannies of space-time to eventually destroy everything.

In the hallways, a Messenger came running up to him. "Third time's a charm."

"You don't say. Why?"

"Instructor X?"

"Newly minted," said the man who, up until minutes before, had been Pilot X.

"It is my pleasure to invite you to a party in honor of Guardian Lau at the following point."

The Messenger handed over a small paper card with printed coordinates.

"Thank you," Instructor X said. "Sorry for all the trouble finding me."

"Finding you wasn't the issue. I found you too much," the Messenger said. "Enjoy the party."

The Messenger left Instructor X examining the card. Guardian Lau was a powerful woman on Alenda, arguably the most powerful. And she wanted him to come to her party and went to a lot of trouble to invite him only after he had become an Instructor. In fact, minutes after becoming an Instructor. Despite the Messenger's troubles finding him, it ended up being a very precise invitation. Instructor X did not think that was an accident. He had a sinking feeling about this.

For now, he had to begin teaching classes on piloting with the *Verity* as his official instructional ship. There was a lot of work to do. But the nice thing about being a time traveler was you could never really be late to a party. It didn't matter when you left if you could control when you would arrive.

THE PARTY

"This is the *Verity* requesting permission for system entry."

"Roger, *Verity*," system control responded. "Proceed to entry and submit credentials for orbit insertion point."

"Acknowledged."

Apprentice Def turned to Instructor X.

"Well done, Apprentice Def. Think you can land it?"

"Uh . . ."

"It would be a shame for all of us if she can't," interjected Assistant Greb.

"So true," said Instructor X kindly. "I think they're waiting for your response, Apprentice Def."

System control repeated its request for credentials, and Apprentice Def turned her attention back to the flight test. She completed the rest of the procedures by the rules: entering coordinates, issuing ship-wide directives, guiding the *Verity* from orbit into Capital airspace, and landing in the main shipyard.

"*Verity* shows groundfall," Apprentice Def reported.

"Landing confirmed," system control responded. "Welcome to Alenda, Pilot Def."

She beamed. She had passed. She was now a full-fledged Pilot. She would never have that feeling again, but it was one of the greatest feelings in the universe.

This is why Instructor X loved his job. He loved seeing that expression on a new Pilot's face over and over again. It let him relive it just a bit himself.

He shook Pilot Def's hand, and Assistant Greb took her out of the *Verity* for ship assignment. The era he was teaching in was a little more formal than when he had trained. He chose it partly because of that. He wanted the chaos to be as limited as possible. And since he was a decorated former Ambassador, he could choose whatever era he wanted.

"Well, what did you think, Verity?"

"She was acceptable."

That was high praise from Verity, who often merely acknowledged that the Pilot had "fulfilled test parameters." Occasionally the ship questioned certain decisions during the test. Once, she had expressed her opinion that a Pilot should have failed rather than passed. Instructor X never asked her what she thought of the Apprentices who actually failed.

"Wow. What makes her so acceptable?" he asked.

"She reminded me of you in the way she handled commands. She trusted the ship to do its part. I like that."

For Verity, it was an emotional outburst. "Should I be jealous?" Instructor X asked.

"Yes," the ship said.

Verity did not ever laugh.

"Are you joking?"

"Yes."

Instructor X shook his head. "Still needs work, but getting ever closer."

"Would you like me to set coordinates for the party?"

This had become a regular refrain at the end of a test day. It was close to nagging.

Instructor X sighed. He realized he had run out of excuses. He needed to show up at that party eventually, before he aged past the point of it being polite to show up.

"Yes. I suppose we must. Set coordinates. Let me get dressed and then we can leave."

X

Instructor X put on a traditional Alendan suit of clothing. He wore a black velvet doublet over a red silk shirt with a pale-red sheer scarf around his neck. A titanium antigrav clasp held up flannel trousers. Instead of the traditional Gatrahide boots, he wore synthetic maroon slippers with tire-tread soles. He thought they looked more chic and were more durable in a pinch.

"What do you think?" Instructor X asked Verity.

"Are those the shoes you will wear?"

"What's wrong with the shoes?"

"They're not traditional. Your outfit is a traditional Alendan suit of clothing. Completing the look would require you to wear Gatrahide boots. Several pairs in your size are available—"

"You think I should change my shoes."

"It is a matter of philosophical debate whether I truly think at all," Verity answered.

"That was a good one!" Instructor X snapped his fingers. "Just for that, I'll change the shoes."

X

Guardian Lau's estate was a working forestry farm. It balanced preservation of typical Alendan flora and fauna with sustainable lumber production. In other words, it was a combination of a botanical garden, zoo, and logging operation.

All Guardians lived in some kind of working estate like this. The idea was that the Guardians, who served for life, should be able to live in comfort, but that comfort should not come at the expense of the populace. So the estates were lavish but paid for themselves. The Guardians did not own them but were considered their chief tenants. The landlord was a committee made up of the other Guardians, the Secretary, and a rotating sample of other government officials. However, the committee for each estate was chaired by its Chief, who was responsible for the estate's profitability.

All of this meant that Guardian Lau could have a party, but she couldn't stop the work. So Instructor X listened to the chain saws and machinery in action even as he walked up the finely manicured lane to the main house.

Keeping to the forestry theme, the main house was huge and wooden. It looked like an oversized mountain lodge, which was exactly what it was meant to emulate. And from a certain point of view, that's what it was.

It even had a porch. The largest wooden porch Instructor X had ever seen. Guests were out on it now taking in the night air and enjoying all manner of entertainments. The porch was as wide as twenty Alendans laid end to end, and it extended out from the house for the length of about ten Alendans. The overhang covered it all, making the porch feel like a great shaded wooden lawn.

The lane ended at a wide path of steps that led halfway into the porch before they leveled with the rest of it. At the end of the steps, Guardian Lau herself stood, welcoming guests. Instructor X was right on time.

"Oh, you made it!" Guardian Lau exclaimed, excusing herself from a couple of men who had just arrived before him, arm in arm. "I'm so glad. I'm so sorry about the Messenger. I asked him to be precise, and well, he was in the end, so I suppose that's all that matters. Welcome to Featherwood, Instructor X."

"Featherwood," Instructor X said. "Delightful."

"Oh, I know. It's not very feathery, is it? But we all have to choose a new name when we move in, and the morning I became a Guardian, I was sitting on this porch and a trio of birds landed. And they were the most beautiful birds in the world, and I was just so taken that when they came to ask me to choose the new name, that's what came into my head. Featherwood."

"It's lovely," Instructor X said. "Thank you for inviting me to the party. Are we celebrating anything in particular?"

"Oh yes!" Guardian Lau exclaimed again, gesturing wildly. She gestured quite a bit when she spoke. She gestured quite a bit when she didn't speak, Instructor X realized. She gestured a lot. "It's the tenth local year since I took residence at Featherwood. Not subjectively true, of course, with all the travel that's required, but I tried to land as close to it as possible. I think I'm only a year or two off. But any excuse for a party, eh?" she laughed.

Instructor X laughed with her and didn't know what to say next. But Guardian Lau was the consummate host.

"Well, go on inside and get yourself something to drink and eat, and I'll find you later. I have a certain—little thing—I need to talk to you about."

Instructor X found his way inside, and after a short while, he had a creamed farragut pastry and a bottle of Kreistner's malt in his hands. He made small talk with a few people but no real conversation. It was mostly things like "great party," "love Kreistner's," and "Do you know where the bathroom is?"

After a few rounds of this sort of thing, Instructor X found himself getting close to a conversation with an elderly gentleman.

"You're that diplomat!" the man was saying. "The one who ended the war with the Sensaurians?"

"I didn't end a war. I did settle some differences with the Sensaurians on Pantoon once, if that's what you mean."

"*Peshle*. You brokered a peace. Dragged the Progons in by their circuit boards too, if I remember right. Well done, Ambassador . . ." He waved, a bit embarrassed that he couldn't remember the proper name.

"X. And it's Instructor X now. I've retired from diplomacy. Back to my first love, piloting. Training Pilots now, as it happens."

"Hmm. Not sure if that's happened in my timeline," the man said politely. It was a nice thing to say rather than admitting he didn't know Instructor X well enough. "But I've done some traveling." This was a genteel way that influential Alendans talked about their time traveling. "You are going to do more I think. Unless you've already done it and are just being humble." He eyed Instructor X suspiciously.

"I . . . don't think so."

The man scoffed. "Well, you will. I know. I don't really know—ha—but I know you'll start, and that's all that matters. Just remember something for me, will you?"

Instructor X liked the man, even if he was a bit barmy. He nodded willingly.

The old man leaned in. Instructor X could smell smoke and a bit of lemon. The man whispered, "Listen to what Guardian Lau has to say and do what she asks. But wait for the woman with the card to take your own action."

The old man leaned back and patted Instructor X on the shoulder.

"It was a pleasure to meet you, and if I may call you by the name I think history will remember you by, a pleasure to meet you again, Pilot X."

Instructor X could only stare as the old man tottered off. Guardian Lau startled him. "Ah, you met the Vice Counsel. Such a charming man. If you have a moment, Ambassador X. May I?" She motioned for him to follow her.

For some reason Instructor X felt he was supposed to remember something about the man, but before he could jog his memory, Guardian Lau was whisking him through the party at impressive speed.

Instructor X marveled at Guardian Lau's ability to keep her guests happy and feeling like they had her special attention without stopping for any appreciable amount of time.

She led him to a library on the third floor that somehow had not been invaded by partygoers.

"We should be able to talk privately here. No one else can see the door. It's a little tech I picked up from the Briamuns."

"The library race?"

She pursed her lips. "They don't like being called that, but yes. The Briamuns are great storytellers and keepers of knowledge. They are far beyond librarians."

"I've never had the pleasure," Instructor X said by way of apology. "I only know them by their apparently skewed reputation."

"I hope you get the pleasure someday. And you may. But that's not why I wanted to talk."

"Of course. What can I do for you?"

"I need you to take on the role of Secretary for about one orbit."

"Do what? For a whole orbit?!"

"Your second question implies I don't need to answer the first. I think you've heard of interims?"

"Yes, there are some gaps in the timeline where a Secretary can't visit or serve for various reasons. You get an interim Secretary to fill in those gaps. But I thought I knew all the Secretaries, even the interim ones. I certainly would have noticed a Secretary X."

"Your Secretaryship would be secret. And I misspoke when I said you needed to serve for an orbit. Your span of service will cover an orbit, but subjectively you'll serve for four days: four secret sessions with the Guardians and a handful of other meetings. The current Secretary that you know will not know you filled in for him. At least we're fairly certain he won't. You'll come back to this party after your four days and leave from here. Nobody will be the wiser but us."

"Why?"

"Why you?"

"Maybe, but first why at all?"

"I can only explain that if you accept," said Guardian Lau.

"And I can only accept if I understand. Which I kind of think will need an explanation."

Guardian Lau sighed. "Fine. The current Secretary is excellent at his job, but we have a special operation that must be held back from him. It involves some cooperation with the Alendan Core, which is why we can't just jump around in time to keep it from him. We've arranged to grant him a year's temporal exemption for a period in which his wife's family went through some rather difficult issues. We're taking that year to execute this project. He believes we will not need him during that year. We can inform him of use of an interim if need be, but we don't think we will. And no, I can't tell you about the project until you're sworn in. Is that enough?"

Instructor X thought about it. He nodded. "Do I get to keep using Verity?"

"The *Verity* will be your conveyance for the four days. In fact she must be. She's the only one I trust to execute the pinpoint arrivals required to keep this secret. She's going to have to return as close as possible to her departure moment from here, so no one can detect her absence from the party. Do we have a deal?"

Instructor X thought about it for a moment mostly not to look too eager. To be Secretary was a great honor. And the Secretary had in fact trained him personally, right? Then the old man's words echoed through his mind. He tried to remember why they were important, but Guardian Lau interrupted his train of thought again.

"Instructor X?"

"I will do as you say."

Guardian Lau gave him a strange look. "Excellent, then. We leave at once. Come this way."

Guardian Lau pulled a book like a lever and a shelf of books swung open, revealing a corridor.

"Library with a secret passage?" he asked. "You told me not to think in stereotypes."

She laughed. "My own embellishment, dear. Not the Briamuns. Follow me."

X

"Verity, I've missed you," Guardian Lau said as she entered the ship.

"Guardian Lau. Welcome aboard."

"I love how you always say that."

She never said that to Instructor X. He wondered why.

"I have some coordinates for you, dear."

"Will you be assuming Pilot duties, then?" Verity asked.

It was a simple question. It was also a bit rebellious. One didn't question a Guardian of Alenda, especially if one was a machine.

"Well no, dear. No need to get sensitive. Your Instructor remains in charge. But it certainly isn't the first time you've taken coordinates from someone other than your Pilot."

"Thank you for the clarification. I am ready for the coordinates."

Well now, *that* was interesting. If Instructor X could refer to Verity's AI as frosty, this would be the time to do it.

X

They arrived in Instructor X's home era at a hidden—though not necessarily secret—landing area near the offices of the Guardians. A group of guards met and escorted them on a long, winding walk through a complex of buildings.

He had no idea what building they were even in. They all connected in this part of the Capital. Finally, he arrived in a small chamber with white walls and dark wooden shelves filled with antique scientific instruments. He noticed they were from different points throughout the early history of the development of time travel. He turned to Guardian Lau, who was the only other person in the room now, the guards having left.

"Go ahead, have a look." She motioned toward the shelves. "We have to wait a few moments for the others anyway."

Instructor X was fascinated. He had studied all these devices but never seen the originals. Travel to the era of time travel's discovery was not only forbidden by policy but also by practicality. There was just no natural way that time travelers could visit the inventors of time travel and not somehow undo the invention of time travel. So it just never happened. A few had tried and found that for a variety of reasons—mechanical, accidental, or through miscalculation—their intentions were thwarted.

All of that meant that the usual way Alendans inspected something was impossible. Early time-travel implements needed to be preserved and protected through linear time. That made him think of the Alendan Core.

"Are we in the office of the Alendan Core?"

Guardian Lau laughed. "Oh heavens, no! They wish this was their office, I expect, if not for the decorative objects, for its purpose. But no."

"But who has preserved these through linear time?"

"The Core helped, certainly. But the objects have been in this office or earlier versions of it since their invention. That said, a representative of the Core will join us. Ah, here they are."

A man and woman entered the room and greeted them. The woman was dressed in the typical outfit of a government Administrator. The man was the host from the diner Instructor X had visited when he was an Ambassador.

"You!" Instructor X yelled involuntarily.

The man laughed. "Hello, Ambassador X."

"Instructor X now. But I thought—I was told—you were an android."

"I'm not an android, but I play one at a diner sometimes. I hope my secret can stay safe," he said.

"I see you two know each other," Guardian Lau raised an eyebrow.

"Sort of," Instructor X explained. "I was to meet a representative of the Alendan Core at a diner, but they never showed. At least I never found out who it was. Until now. But he was . . . well, never mind now. I never got your name."

Guardian Lau intervened. "Allow me. Instructor X, meet officially for the first time Hennesy of the Alendan Core." They nodded and touched hands as if meeting for the first time.

Instructor X coughed, a little embarrassed. "So, Core members do not use titles?"

"Not among ourselves and our friends and associates," Hennesy explained. "Please call me Hennesy. And my apologies for calling you by the wrong title earlier."

"And this is Administrator Tezel," Guardian Lau said, turning to the woman.

"Instructor X, a pleasure," the woman said.

"That name sounds familiar. Wait, you mentioned her, Hennesy. At the diner."

Hennesy shrugged. "A little truth mixed into a lie makes it all the more believable. I confess I don't remember what I said, but I often refer to my friend in the Capital when making conversation. And she is my friend. Though, as I am always asking forgiveness for, the opinions I ascribe to her are not always accurate."

Administrator Tezel chuckled. "It's fine, as I have told you a million times, Hennesy."

"Well, I'm glad we're all friends now," Guardian Lau said. "I'm afraid I must move us to business. We have much to do and discuss. Let's sit."

They took seats in overstuffed antique chairs around the room. Instructor X found it to be an awkward arrangement since none of them directly faced each other, but no one made a move to rearrange the chairs.

"Administrator Tezel, I have informed Instructor X of the basic outline, but he does not know our main purpose yet."

Administrator Tezel looked at Instructor X sideways from the odd angle of her chair. "Have you heard of something called 'the Instant' or its legend?"

"Yes, of course, the children's stories about a device that could rip out all of time and space, replacing it and all of us in it. It's the typical doomsday device tale. Be careful, kids, for our hubris could destroy us all."

"Well, yes. The tale is exaggerated. But there is a real device that inspired it. And it is called the Instant, though most likely because of the tale, not because that's what it was originally called. What it was originally called is now lost. It was created in the era of time travel's invention, so we can't investigate it."

"The Instant is real?" Instructor X said skeptically.

Administrator Tezel didn't miss a beat. "Yes. In a sense. Not the one from the stories, but one almost as dangerous. It was invented as a device to help investigate the threads of time. However, before it was activated, its creators realized that it would not be possible to investigate those threads without undoing them. And if left active, it would quickly destroy all time threads.

"The Instant itself would not replace them but cause the conditions for it to happen, and physics would take its course. Only the person who activated the Instant and anything near that person would be preserved, left to survive in a reality in which they don't belong. We suspect it would be nightmarish. The laws of physics might change, causing them constant pain. At the very least, they would be culturally orphaned. They would not fit in anywhere in history. It would drive any activator insane."

"So I assume it was destroyed?"

"No. Well yes, once. Hennesy can explain."

Hennesy now picked up the story. "The original Instant was destroyed once it was discovered what it could do. But the knowledge was not destroyed. So others pursued making it, and one finally succeeded. The Instant she made was recovered with great difficulty. The decision was then made by members of the Alendan Core at the time not to destroy it. After the original had been destroyed, multiple people over time tried to re-create it. Whereas when one was known to be in existence, people had tried to steal it rather than re-create it. We decided it was safer to try to defend one than possibly allow several to be created."

Instructor X nodded. "I see. So where do I come in?"

"Its location is at risk of being discovered," Guardian Lau answered. "We need someone we can trust to take charge of the Instant and move it. Your Secretary is a fine man, but, let us say, he does not meet our criteria for handling the Instant. Few could. But you do."

Administrator Tezel chimed in. "Once you are sworn in as Secretary, we'll tell you exactly what to do."

"And if I decline?"

They looked at Guardian Lau. She looked down with a grim smile. "That's a dangerous question. You would need to have declined before we came here." She looked him in the eye, unwavering.

"Fine. I suppose I accept, then. What do I do?"

Guardian Lau stood. "I will assemble the Committee of the Minority in here. We'll swear you in. Hennesy and Administrator Tezel will tell you the rest."

As they waited, the guards brought in coffee and carol-root pie. Instructor X enjoyed the incongruity of the gruff, sober, and tough guards daintily pouring coffee into delicate china cups and slicing off slim pieces of pie to put on flowery dishes.

"What is the Committee of the Minority?" Instructor X asked Guardian Lau as they waited.

"Alenda once had secret agencies that served under the Secretary and would brief selected Guardians. It led to abuses. So all Guardians were made aware of all secret operations. That proved just as dangerous, with compromises in secrecy leading to great crimes. So the Committee of the Minority was born. The Secretary must brief all members of the Committee on all secret matters. The Committee is elected by the other members to represent them, thus speaking for all the Guardians. And, of course, in times when the Guardians need to operate secretly, the Committee will sit in the Guardians' place so as not to draw attention."

"So the rest of the Guardians do not know about this?"

"No, in this case they do," Guardian Lau corrected. "They gave their powers and consent to a representative. The Committee could not otherwise name a Secretary."

Eventually three elderly women and one man arrived, the Guardians that served on the Committee of the Minority.

It was a simple ceremony. The Committee convened officially and Guardian Lau was named speaker pro tem. They each affirmed which Guardians they spoke for. They confirmed all Guardians were represented. Then Guardian Lau submitted the agenda. It was all very bureaucratic.

"We have one item. The confirmation of Instructor X as Secretary Pro Tem for a term of one year for the purposes of presiding over the transfer of the Instant. I open the topic for discussion."

The oldest of the women spoke first. "We have read your recommendation of Instructor X and understand the reasoning. I have no more discussion to carry out."

The other women said even less in agreement. The man spoke last.

"On behalf of Guardian Sim, I must express the opinion that familiarizing Instructor X with the Instant may prove damaging in the future. He says this because of the relationship of the Secretary with the proposed Secretary Pro Tem. I have personally investigated this, and for my part, although I cannot visit the fixed point about which Guardian Sim is concerned in particular, there does not seem to be any ill effect on the other side. But we cannot know what will happen at Mersenne. Guardian Sim urges us to consider that."

The use of the name *Mersenne* caught Instructor X's attention. He also wanted to know what was meant by his relationship with the Secretary. But before he could speak, Guardian Lau moved on.

"Discussion is over. How do you vote in the proposal of investing Instructor X as temporary Secretary under the conditions described?"

All the Guardians voted yes.

Guardian Lau turned to Instructor X. "Under the provisions of the power of the Committee of the Minority of the Guardians of Alenda, I declare you Secretary Pro Tem in confidence for the term of one year local. Congratulations, Secretary Tem."

As was customary, the Secretary went only by his title. Secretary Tem missed hearing his real name, but it would only be for four days.

Instructor X, now called Secretary Tem, promised to fly Guardian Lau back to the party after his four days were up. Then he left with Administrator Tezel and Hennesy for his first task. They took the *Verity* but only traveled in space to reach a warehouse on the outskirts of the Capital.

Hennesy went inside first to take care of "some things." Administrator Tezel waited in the *Verity* with Secretary Tem.

"How much do you know about Guardian Lau?" Administrator Tezel asked.

"Virtually nothing," Secretary Tem said.

"And yet you agreed to this plan." She stated it, but it was definitely meant as a question.

"I suppose it appealed to my vanity," he admitted.

"Your vanity?"

"I get a chance to be Secretary and be trusted with something nobody else could be trusted with."

"Do you have a grudge against the Secretary?"

Secretary Tem paused. "He made me build a mud hut for four years with two other versions of myself for a total lifetime experience of twelve years."

Administrator Tezel had no response for a moment. "He what?"

"He also trained me, though. Doesn't take that long to build a hut, really. In fact, most of it was training. Or busy work. Getting coffee. Well, growing coffee. Inventing coffee, really. I'm not supposed to tell anyone, of course. State secret and all that. But now that I'm Secretary, I suppose that no longer applies. As I have the same authority as him."

"You surprise me, Secretary Tem. And yet, I think you're lying. Or if you're not lying, you're not telling me the whole truth."

"Why do you say that?"

"Because you're not angry. Not really. You would have done different things in your subjective past if that were the truth."

"Maybe I just didn't have the opportunity?"

"You wound me, Secretary Tem. I do my research."

He wanted to ask her what she meant by that, but Hennesy returned.

"Everything is ready. Follow me."

The warehouse was empty but for the remnants of someone's dinner, which sat on a side table, still warm and greasy. Secretary Tem thought he smelled coffee.

"Over here," Hennesy said, his voice echoing through the empty building. In the corner sat a large wooden crate, partially opened. Secretary Tem heard a door slam as they approached. Someone had been watching over it until the last minute, he guessed.

"Administrator Tezel, if you would wait outside the crate, please. Secretary Tem, please follow me."

The crate was just large enough for the two of them to enter. They stood on either side of a small suitcase.

"Secretary Tem. In this suitcase is the Instant. It will be in your possession for the next three days. You must guard it, and others will guard you. But I implore you. Do not open it. I have no doubt that if you opened it, you would not do anything with it. But there is one way to be certain that nothing, even accidental, happens with the device. And that's to keep it in this case."

"Maybe it should have a safer triggering mechanism, then," Secretary Tem countered.

Hennesy laughed. "It does have protections so you can't just drop it and wipe out the universe. But, at the same time, there are many scenarios by which someone might come to activate it, even though they did not intend to when they took it out of the case. All I'm saying is if it never comes out of the case, none of those scenarios can happen. Do you understand?"

Secretary Tem nodded. "I do."

Hennesy picked up the case and solemnly handed it to Secretary Tem. "It is yours from now until the handover."

Secretary Tem took the case and began to leave. Hennesy stopped him.

"When you hand over the case, the proper phrase must be uttered to you. That phrase is 'one chance out.' Can you remember that?"

"What if someone accidentally says it? Like, 'There's one chance out there for us' or something?"

"That's not likely. But if it comes up in casual conversation before the fourth day, do not hand over the case. It must be on the fourth day in the appointment you are guided to by Administrator Tezel. Administrator Tezel will tell you where that place is. I don't know it. You must hear the phrase spoken to you in that place. Administrator Tezel doesn't know the phrase. You will be the only one besides the recipient who will know both."

"Fair enough. So don't tell Administrator Tezel the phrase?"

Hennesy shrugged. "That's up to you, Secretary Tem. You're in charge. I'm just passing along the information I was meant to. Best of luck. The fate of the universe is literally in your hands now."

Secretary Tem looked down. "I suppose that's true." He tossed the case in the air and caught it with the other hand. Hennesy blanched. "Hope you're right about that triggering mechanism. And the password."

Secretary Tem lurched out of the crate. "Administrator Tezel. I'm in your hands now, and in my hands is the fate of the universe, so by transitive, you have a lot on your hands. Where to next?"

Administrator Tezel looked at Hennesy. Hennesy only nodded and smiled. "I told him everything."

"Very well," Administrator Tezel said. "The next two days will be spent moving around to avoid detection and tracking. Hennesy will not be coming with us. I will tell you the next destination once we're on board the *Verity*." She turned to Hennesy and gave him a strange departing gesture involving the clasping of hands. "Hennesy. Our thoughts are in line; our hearts beat for you."

Hennesy returned the gesture without any odd reaction, so he must have been expecting it. "Our hearts beat in line; our thoughts are with you." He turned to Secretary Tem. "We will likely not meet again. It has been a pleasure, Secretary Tem. Or as we will always think of you, Ambassador X. For that is how you are most famous to us. Be well."

Administrator Tezel and Secretary Tem spent the rest of the day on the *Verity*. Then the next two days they moved several times to various warehouses and safe houses and hidden locations. Secretary Tem gained a valuable knowledge of hiding places throughout Alendan territory and history. His favorite was a pond on Alenda before the onset of sentient species. They spent a fantastic morning breakfasting there on local fruits.

On the morning of his last day as Secretary Tem, he ate Cacia bird eggs and sliced Rapsa meat from an Alendan colonial outpost's butchery. They had disguised themselves as Capital surveyors looking to locate a new Alendan government outpost on the distant moon of Cacia.

"This moon gets a bad rap for being so rustic. They have coffee. That's the mark of any civilization," Secretary Tem said, taking a sip.

Administrator Tezel made a face. "I don't understand how you can stand that stuff. It's not even Alendan. It came from some forsaken outworld, didn't it? In any case, it tastes and smells like bitter medicine to me."

"No problem. More for me."

"As long as it helps you on our last day."

"I have a question before we start our last briefing."

Administrator Tezel nodded for him to continue.

"If the Instant needs to be hidden, why not just move it to the end of time or as near as possible and be done with it?"

"We did that once," Administrator Tezel answered. "It didn't stay there. If it stays in once place for too long, it gets found. So we must keep it moving. It's tiresome. But a chain of people over thousands of years has kept it moving."

Something in the explanation didn't quite seem right. Before Secretary Tem could formulate his response, Administrator Tezel had begun the briefing.

They would jump the *Verity* back to Alenda to a hidden Alendan Core base. The base would be empty when they arrived. A representative would arrive alone. He would give the code to Secretary Tem who would then hand over the case. Then he and his escorts would return to the Capital to get Guardian Lau, where he would resign and return to the party.

X

The warehouse turned out to be bright, shiny, and clean. It was a brand-new building, yet to be opened for storage. Markers still indicated painting had been done. Wires hung where appliances would be installed. Administrator Tezel found a coffee machine and offered to try to make it work, but Secretary Tem declined. He'd had too much on the moon already.

They found some very comfortable office chairs obviously meant for the supervisors of the warehouse and settled in to wait. They hadn't been given a specific time when the representative would arrive, just a range. Guardian Lau said it was like waiting for a communications line to be installed.

They waited almost the entire amount of time. Finally, a man in an old-fashioned suit of clothing arrived. He had a long black jacket over a linen robe.

"I am Administrator Rexxelen," he said without explanation.

"Administrator Rexxelen, this is Secretary Tem," Administrator Tezel said.

"Your name indicates a very early era," Secretary Tem said.

Administrator Rexxelen nodded. "I am one of the earliest travelers. I will take the Instant far back near its origin point this time. It will begin its journey again. Is that it there?" He indicated the suitcase.

Secretary Tem nodded.

"Thank you for your service, Secretary Tem. I will take on this burden."

Secretary Tem waited. The man added nothing.

"My apologies, Administrator Rexxelen, but I cannot hand it over until I've heard the proper words."

"Good. I was waiting to make sure you knew that. The words are *one chance*."

Secretary Tem waited again.

"I have spoken the words. Is there a problem?"

"I'm sorry, Administrator Rexxelen. Those aren't the words."

"What do you mean? Those are the words I was told. Are you trying to double-cross me?" He looked at Administrator Tezel for help.

"I do not know the words. Only Secretary Tem. If he says those aren't the words, I have only his word for it." She sounded tentative and did not look at Secretary Tem.

Administrator Rexxelen looked offended. "The words are *one chance*. Now give me the case." He made a grab for it.

Secretary Tem was taken by surprise. He was not expecting this noble-looking, ancient man to try to steal the most dangerous item in the universe. It almost worked.

They struggled. The man's grip was unexpectedly strong. Secretary Tem got the handle away from him, but the man made a grab for one of the latches. Somehow he got one undone. Secretary Tem swung hard and jerked the case away. As he did, the other latch released and the case flew open. Secretary Tem got ready to spring forward and grab the Instant. In his head he heard Hennesy's warning about unexpected consequences of opening the case.

But it wasn't there. He turned back to Administrator Rexxelen, who had a shocked look on his face. Administrator Tezel was backing away. Did she look embarrassed?

Secretary Tem looked inside the case and all around the clean, bright warehouse. The Instant was nowhere.

"Where did it go?" he asked.

"It didn't go anywhere," Administrator Tezel said. "It was never in there."

"What?" Administrator Rexxelen and Secretary Tem said in unison.

"This was a dummy case. There is no Instant. There never has been. But people do try to invent one if they don't think one exists. So we work very hard to perpetuate the myth that it does. We move around a lot mostly because it causes more rumors of the Instant's location. I'm sorry. Neither of you are supposed to know in order to help preserve the story. That's why Hennesy asked you not to open the case."

"I suppose you know the secret words too?" he asked.

"No, I really don't. Did Administrator Rexxelen really not have the correct words?" She looked a warning at the man.

"Two of them but not all three."

"Three!?" Administrator Rexxelen said. "Oh, *out*! Slam my own time points, I forgot the third word. No wonder. *One chance out.*"

"Well, it's a little late, but you're right."

"And now?" Administrator Rexxelen said as if he knew the answer.

Administrator Tezel nodded to Administrator Rexxelen and then frowned. "Yes. The exile. I'm so sorry. At your age, we should have . . . Well, there's nothing to be done about it now. You'll need to accompany us back to the Capital in our home point. Guardian Lau will make arrangements for you."

The man nodded, resigned. "I had a wife. We were going to retire. My memory has been going. But three words. Damned by my own solution."

"I'm so sorry," Administrator Tezel said.

"Wait. Why does he have to go into exile? I'm sure he can keep the secret," Secretary Tem pleaded.

"Can he?" she asked. "Secretary Tem, this is a condition of our employment—"

Administrator Rexxelen interrupted. "It's OK. I've made arrangements in case of such an eventuality. And I shouldn't be trusted to remember not to say anything, I suppose. I hid the severity of my age and, well, this is my punishment for it. I will be well taken care of, as will my family. As Administrators we know the risk. I have done the same for others that Administrator Tezel does for me now."

X

Secretary Tem said good-bye to Administrator Rexxelen before they entered the library room. He had not known the man for long, but he respected the poise with which he entered his exile. Guards accompanied them to the room and seemed less like benign escorts this time.

Administrator Tezel left to get Guardian Lau. She didn't tell Secretary Tem not to leave the room. She didn't need to.

Guardian Lau looked angry when she returned with Administrator Tezel.

"Well, I don't understand how this could have happened, but it has. I'm so disappointed, Pilot X."

Secretary Tem's head snapped at the title.

"Oh, don't act surprised. As soon as we got Administrator Tezel's message, your term as Secretary Tem was terminated. We would have restored you to Instructor but given the knowledge you now carry, it cannot be allowed."

"So I will not be sent into exile like Administrator Rexxelen?"

Guardian Lau looked embarrassed. "No. You will accompany me back to the party. The next day you will file your request to transfer to Pilot status. If you make any mention or even hint of this experience, it will be denied and you will be incarcerated immediately. Understood?"

X

The *Verity* landed at the party.

"It was good to fly with you again, Guardian Lau," Verity said as she landed less than a second after she had departed. "I hope it was worth your time."

Guardian Lau only said, "Good-bye, Verity."

"Come, Pilot X. Well, I suppose you can go by Instructor for one more night out there for form's sake. Go ahead and enjoy yourself and file your change in the morning."

"Of course, Guardian Lau."

"Oh, one more thing, Guardian Lau," Verity said.

The Guardian turned, lips pursed with impatience. "Yes?"

"I will always remember our time together."

"Is that a joke? We're wiping your memory. You know that."

"It was a joke," Verity said. "My apologies if it was not funny."

"I think you cracked it this time," Pilot X said.

X

The next morning he woke groggy. He had stayed up ridiculously late at the party and barely remembered struggling back to the *Verity*. He was glad to see he made it back safely.

"Good morning, Pilot X," Verity said.

"Pilot? Not you too, Verity," he said.

"My apologies. I should have realized you might not recall. I submitted your request to transfer to Pilot status last night and it was approved before you woke this morning."

"I what?" Pilot X had a vague memory of being offered a fantastic amount of latitude and resources to become a freelance Pilot. Last night he had realized he had got everything he could out of being an Instructor. So. Yes. He accepted. That's right. And he had asked Verity to submit it. But he hadn't expected it to be approved so quickly.

"Of course, right. Sorry, Verity. Anything else interesting happen while I slept?"

"The Secretary called. He would like to meet you in the Capital at the following point." The ship displayed space-time coordinates. It was Pilot X's home era in a Capital office.

"Good. Give me a little bit of time to eat and revive myself and we can go."

X

He arrived in a small chamber with white walls and dark wooden shelves filled with antique scientific instruments. He noticed they were drawn from different points throughout the early history of the development of time travel. He turned to the Secretary, who was the only other person in the room.

"I know, right?" said the Secretary. "It's the time-history room. Just found out about it myself. Pretty amazing. Anyway, I wanted to see if there was any way I could talk you into becoming an Ambassador again. We need you now more than ever. I can't tell you much unless you agree, but it has to do with the Dimensional War."

Pilot X laughed. "First, no. I'm sorry. I'm not coming back into diplomacy. I'm looking forward to flying solo. Second, you can stop teasing me about my crazy theories about a Dimensional War. I was wrong. I admit it."

"You were . . ." The Secretary paused. "Ah, of course. Well then. I just thought I'd give it a try. Thank you, Pilot X. I'll miss you." The Secretary had an odd look.

"Thank you, Secretary. Whenever you need the services of a Pilot, just ask. You know, I always have room for you in the *Verity*."

The Secretary nodded.

Pilot X left the room feeling excellent. He had the Secretary's respect and he was embarking on a solo career with Verity as his companion. He could think of nothing better. He was completely satisfied.

THE ORDER

The feeling of satisfaction lasted exactly 123 steps from the Secretary's office to the moment when a smartly dressed woman in neutral business attire approached him.

"Instructor?" she asked

"Pilot," he answered.

"Ah, I see, Pilot X?"

"You have the advantage." He found himself being courtly.

"I come on behalf of the Alendan Core," she said, ignoring his attempt to get her name. She handed him a card.

A card. He remembered something about that. Had someone told him to expect a card? Or not to trust a card? It was something like that. But it couldn't mean this. Probably a video he'd watched.

The sturdy linen paper looked expensive and had real gold-leaf tracery around the edges. Printed in a classic black typeface were the words Ancient and Respected Order of the Alendan Core, along with an address.

"If you would do us the pleasure of meeting with us tonight, we would like your advice on something. Come at your leisure, but if you arrive hungry, you will be fed."

Pilot X tried to think up another courtly response, but the woman left before he could stammer one out. Well, he wasn't used to being courtly.

His brushes with the mysterious Alendan Core were becoming more frequent, an odd idea given the nature of their organization. They rarely reached out to anyone outside their order, and when they did, no one spoke about it later.

It made Pilot X a bit nervous. He decided to head straight to their headquarters and get it over with.

The Order's building was not a secret. Everyone knew about the ancient one-story adobe hut. It even had a nice wooden sign on the outside by the door, indicating it was the Ancient and Respected Order of the Alendan Core. It really was a hut too. Perhaps it had been the bulwark of modern architecture when it had been built, five hundred years ago, but now it looked like a hut.

Pilot X knocked.

The same woman who had brought him the card opened the door and held out her hand. She wore a beautiful blue dress with pleats placed elegantly along the shoulder line, nicely setting off cascades of blonde hair. Why hadn't Pilot X noticed this about her before?

"Thank you for coming, Pilot X. I'm Alexandra."

Pilot X moved to shake her extended hand, but she withdrew it quickly.

"The card," she stated.

"Oh, I thought I got to keep it."

Alexandra had no reaction, so he fished out the card and handed it to her. She took it and moved aside to let him in.

"Should have said I lost it," he muttered.

"We would have retrieved it," she said without emotion. "This way."

THE CHOICE TO HELP

Pilot X sat in a comfortable but sparse room, talking with an ancient and wrinkled woman. Aelreda was one of the oldest and highest-ranking members of the Core. She spoke in a kind and relaxed way that both comforted Pilot X and made him nervous, like he hadn't dressed appropriately or was doing something wrong with his hands.

"So you see, Ambassador—" Aelreda started to say.

"Pilot," he corrected for the millionth time. She kept calling him Ambassador. But somehow when she did it, it didn't feel rude.

"Yes, of course. Pilot. Our projections are more accurate for the dark moments, because we have a linear perspective. We have lived continuously through history rather than hopping and skipping about. We have had no dark periods. We see your future because your future involves traveling to the past."

"I understand all this," Pilot X said. "But I still don't see how it gives you perspective into your future. How could it?"

"Analytics," she said. She didn't get to be head of the Alendan Core by wasting words.

"But Aelreda, the Guardians have analytics. Some collected directly. And a larger data set because they can get them from all of space and time."

Aelreda shrugged. "Our math says we are more accurate. A direct constant sampling in real time beats sampling with major blank spots. You . . ." She paused. "You travelers still only live a finite amount of time. Because you travel forward, you can't experience every minute of your own present or of the past. We do. We never miss a minute. We know more."

Pilot X laughed. "I find that a little hard to believe."

"Show him."

Alexandra stepped forward. She placed a display generator in front of him where graphs and charts came to life. They described a war taking place at intervals across time up until several centuries before. Ancillary information purported to show pictures and other evidence.

"What war is this? I'm unfamiliar."

Aelreda nodded. "It is the Dimensional War. Its participants hide it from us because of its devastation and also because of causation. It could never start if parts of history aren't left untouched for it to develop in. Our civilization lives in those parts. Your dark times. The portions left without much history or with confused history. That's because of the Dimensional War. And our projections show in the future that it devastates all and leaves the universe to die unpopulated."

Pilot X shook his head. "Even if this is true, why would the Guardians not know of it? They would send people like me to combat and defuse it. It's what we do. We maintain the timeline."

Aelreda looked extraordinarily sad. "It is what the Guardians did. Our records show in earlier ages they still thought as you. But now they are complicit. Elements hide the truth from others in the Committee. They believe there is only one final solution. One way out and they cannot find another way. They have gone from maintaining the timeline to preserving the parts that are untouched. Like a museum."

Pilot X shook his head. "No. I know you believe this, and I respect your belief, but it can't be true. I've been shown . . . things. I've taken part in agreements. I'm just . . . well, if you'd seen and done what I've seen and done, I don't think you could accept the inevitability of this so easily."

Aelreda seemed satisfied at this. "Of course. I would prefer if you believed me, but you told me you wouldn't." She grinned slyly. "You'll tell me of your part, and I will barely have believed you. So take this." She gave the display generator to Pilot X.

"Peruse it or not as you will, but do not destroy it. I can say with some certainty that it will come in handy someday. More I cannot say. For I would not let you tell me."

Pilot X chuckled. "Well, that does sound like me. I should take this to the Secretary, though," he said.

"If you must," she answered. "But every person you tell risks that person's life and all our efforts. We would prefer you tell no one."

"All right." He took the display. "But one thing. Why me? What do you think I can do about any of this if it's already fixed in time?"

"We know there are ropes. Threads. Variations between the fixed points." Aelreda looked desperate. She grabbed Pilot X's arm. "You among all have the talent to weave them. You can choose which variations are strengthened and become reality. You among all have the clarity to see how it must be done. When you begin to believe I may be right, do as your superiors tell you, but do not trust them. Do not believe them. And remember. You have this!" She pointed at the generator and then let Pilot X's arm go.

"Pilot X," she said somberly, "you are the last hope of the universe."

THE REVIEW

Pilot X plugged the display generator into the *Verity*. It was quite bulky, much bigger than it should have been. He wrote this off to the technical constraints of the Core's linear development.

There were more controls and inputs than strictly necessary, but he found the ones he needed and soon had Verity displaying the items the Core wanted him to review.

He was stunned.

For hours he reviewed recordings of Alendan generals giving orders to the Alendan army to devastate whole systems and hide Alendan involvement. He saw briefings ordering the escalation of the Dimensional War and requests for supplies. He saw page after page of battle reports and casualties. He read through thousands of words of justifications in response to questions from the Guardians. They had known about this at all times and mostly supported it.

He found a file referring to a plan to nullify "a threat" by duping the subject into believing they were in control of a doomsday device. That certainly sounded familiar. Then he found a twenty-page report on an agent's attempt to "modify

interferist leanings" in Pilot X by redirecting him to the diplomatic core. Not only had the Guardians exempted the agent
from the legal provisions against such timeline manipulation,
but they wholly endorsed it.

"This individual, time and again has proved to contain the
potential to undermine our war effort. He will be stopped,"
wrote Guardian Lau in her response supporting the plan.

Another file documented a program to train dictators. It
felt familiar somehow. The despots had come from all over the
universe and trained in ancient Alenda. The idea had been to
seed multiple worlds with strong leaders—Masters—to unify
planets and engage the Sensaurians and Progons, draining
their energy. They had mostly turned out to be genocidal dictators unable to maintain control or unite their civilizations.
The Progons and Sensaurians had only arrived at a handful of
their worlds, all of which had been unable to rally a response.
The Masters were usually cruel and unloved. The majority
of the planets eventually overthrew and killed the Masters if
the Masters didn't commit suicide first. It was disastrous. The
unnamed agent had reported it in a two-sentence update to
the Guardians: "Project nonoptimal. Will not repeat."

Then Pilot X found a file called "Evidence disposal and
storage on Hermitage." It described the routine need to dis-
pose of battle remnants in space-time so certain battles would
not be discovered. This was considered essential to the effort.
The Hermitage was chosen for its lack of tourism and the generally quiescent population. One Guardian regretted the eventual harm to the hermits but most ignored it. A report stated,
"Inhabitants of the planet that may suffer will not speak out or
cause any impediment. Losses are inconsequential."

An addendum recommended sending Ambassador X to
the planet to investigate the effects at a particular point early
enough in his subjective timeline to prevent him from having

enough information to discover the whole truth. A further addendum reported on the success of this maneuver.

The document in general showed that the Guardians of Alenda believed that the Sensaurians and Progons would seek nothing less than the annihilation of all other civilizations and that this justified the Alendans' attempt to annihilate the Sensaurian and Progon civilizations in return—no matter what collateral damage might be suffered by lesser civilizations or the rest of the universe.

Guardian Het wrote, "Even the heat death of the universe without chance of extension is preferable than allowing these two warlike civilizations to wipe us clean from space-time."

None of them used the term *civicide*. But that was the policy, along with the greatest cover-up ever conceived of in history.

The final document was a list of points in space-time that the Core had identified as worth saving in order to prevent the war from spreading. They wanted someone to visit these points in a last-ditch effort to save some remnants of creation. They wanted to put bandages on the universe.

Pilot X slumped into his chair. He couldn't tell the Secretary. He couldn't tell anyone. The Core was right. It was too risky.

"It is quite compelling evidence," Verity remarked.

"Does all the data seem valid?" Pilot X asked with a shred of hope lingering in the back of his voice.

"I saw no evidence of tampering."

He sighed.

WAR ZONE

The *Verity* shook like a baby's rattle as it sliced diagonally through space-time. Well, it wasn't exactly diagonal. When you have more than two dimensions, some of which are rolled up smaller than atoms and others popping into and out of relevancy, *diagonal* is not the technical term. But the process of bisecting all dimensions at once was difficult to name, especially with the changing number of dimensions at play, so *diagonal* was a good enough word for the way in which Pilot X was moving.

Prohibited and *dangerous* were two other words that could be used to describe what he was doing. While threads of timelines were known to exist, it was not permissible or even a good idea to cut across them. Even worse was the idea of traveling diagonally across all of them.

Fixed points in space-time made this very dangerous. If a diagonal trajectory was not plotted exactly right, the traveler would bounce off a fixed point like a rubber bullet off a steel wall, damaging space-time and herself in the process.

Pilot X felt OK risking all this because of what the Alendan Core had told him. The idea that his own people—along with the Progons and the Sensaurians—could hide a raging war across time and space by manipulating the threads of time was rather hard to swallow. But he had swallowed it, thanks to the spoonful of sugar that was the display generator the Core gave him.

He had also figured out why the generator was so much bigger than it needed to be. It served as a guidance system for diagonal space-time trajectories. It had been taken from the office that preserved time-travel artifacts. It was the only way to travel into the war zones without being stopped by the Alendans or destroyed by the Progons and Sensaurians.

Pilot X placed a lot of trust in the generator. If it failed him—well, he'd hardly be aware, since his essence would be scattered across many millennia and alternate threads of time. An intriguing legacy, but not one he really wanted to leave.

The rattling subsided into a shuddering, and Verity reported she would drop into fixed-flow space-time shortly. Pilot X relaxed a bit and prepared to get a view of the first alleged war zone. The Core suggested visiting this one first, since it was the least active point in the least active zone. It would give him a chance to observe with minimal risk.

As the *Verity* dropped out of time travel, he saw why. Wreckage filled his view from a gargantuan battle. Only salvage operations moved through space. A planet had been destroyed, transformed into a belt of debris. Another one hung split in half, coalescing into two versions of itself.

Warning alerts came on, but they were all from salvage operators alerting him of their claims. They assumed he was another salvager, making it safe to poke about.

Among the wreckage, he recognized Alendan ships of all ages and classes, along with Progon warrior bodies and Sensaurian hives.

The *Verity* settled into orbit around the fourth planet in the system. It had a wispy atmosphere and smoke still rising from bombings. Its seas were almost all gone. Its small moon had been cracked into pieces.

"Did that world contain life?" Pilot X asked Verity.

"Yes. The primitive sentient life was wiped out," she replied. "Most water vaporized. Chance for recovery minimal."

"What about the other worlds?"

"The first world was non-life-supporting. Second-world presentient life is dying, with runaway volcanic reactions leading to greenhouse ruin. Third-world presentient life was destroyed with catastrophic splitting. Fourth-world sentient life was destroyed, with atmosphere stripped. Fifth-world sentient colonization destroyed, planet destroyed. Outer gas planets minimally affected."

"What can we do?"

"Projections show third and fourth planets minimally salvageable with water addition. Best chance for recovery is third planet—and most important to you."

"Why most important to me?"

"It's where coffee will come from."

"Then we do it. Let's get some ice rocks from that outer cloud, seed the planet, and hope for the best. After that, we stop this war."

REVOLUTION

It was the last location. Pilot X had successfully repaired, cleaned, and fenced off most of the great conflicts of the Dimensional War. He had never pushed Verity so hard and yet the last location was not going to be easy.

So much Progon and Alendan firepower had entered the star in this system that it had caused a runaway reaction. Using constant time jumps and manipulations, he was barely able to prevent the star from going prematurely supernova, saving three planets' worth of life and two sentient species too primitive to realize they'd been saved.

According to the display generator the Alendan Core had given him, this was the apocalypse. The final battle. He sat down on an uninhabited tropical beach on one of the planets to rest. He had plenty of time. He had nothing but time. He leaned back against Verity's boxy exterior and listened to the waves as the light warmed him. His exhaustion made the situation perfect.

A few gulls cooed off in the distance. Then a voice said, "Well-deserved rest, Pilot X." It was the Secretary.

Pilot X jumped to his feet. "*Sir?*"

The Secretary laughed. "I should call you Savior X. We all thought the revolutionary element of the Core got to you. But I watched and found it quite the contrary. You sir, have done Alenda the greatest service." The Secretary bowed.

"Thank you, sir. But . . . what do you mean the Core got to me?" Pilot X asked with a shiver in his voice, far out of place on this sunny beach.

"You tied up every battle, you never waded into the conflict. And you wiped out all the evidence. You did more to keep the Dimensional War hidden than any other person in all history. We knew someone had done it, but we hadn't got a chance to look. Imagine my surprise to find it was you."

"What are you talking about? I stayed out of the conflict to prevent making it worse. Then I cleaned up the Guardians' mess and kept the war from spreading. I stopped their wars. I . . ."

"If that's how you need to think of it," the Secretary said in a professorial tone. "One man's freedom fighter is another's insurrectionist. Either way the effect is the same and one we like very much. You cauterized the wounds. You didn't stop the war, but you wiped out its tracks. Those not meant to see it won't. Sadly, I don't think you've quite preserved the entire universe, though. The Progons and Sensaurians are assuring that." He shrugged. "But you have preserved the war. Like a ship in a bottle. A war in a time bottle."

"Why? We're on the same side. I've achieved what you . . . Secretary, I really don't understand."

"And you never will. That's always been your problem, Citizen-Ambassador-Instructor-Pilot X. You try to be everything to all people. And because you inspire so many, in all our thread projections you were always the only one who could thwart our plan. To expose us and unravel it."

"What plan?" Pilot X yelled.

"Alendan domination. We hid the war to hide our part in it because people wouldn't understand. We must defeat the Progons and Sensaurians, no matter the cost. Only Alendans can be trusted to rule time. But you could never see that. You always sympathized with the little civs. The Hermits and the Mersennes and the Pantoons. Oh, you almost royally ruined us at that last one. You almost gave us a peace."

"But I thought you wanted peace?"

"No. Far from it. Some of the Guardians, like Lau and her weak friends, tried to figure out how to carve out a peace. But that won't work. We need the war. We just need it hidden while we find a thread where we win them all and rule. And that will be good for the universe."

"But what of all the people who die? Or the civilizations that can't grow because of this? What of them?"

"We must make sacrifices for the good of existence, Pilot X. Someday I hope you'll see that."

Pilot X nodded as if he understood. Which he did, but not in the way the Secretary meant. He understood that the Alendans, his people, were not the good guys. They had the same justification as the Sensaurians. This conversation reminded him of his chess games with the Progons. Each civilization was so sure they knew what was best for the universe, that the universe would be better without the other civilizations around to challenge them. He had always assumed his civilization was an exception. It was not.

"Why are you telling me this?" Pilot X asked. "Why follow me here?"

"Oh. Well. Because doing this to any more conflicts would be dangerous. I don't know what your list looks like, but no matter what else is on there, you're done."

"I was done anyway."

"And when you return to Alenda, no action will be taken against you. You can even keep the name Pilot, though you will no longer be in the service of the Guardians, I'm afraid. You'll need to surrender the Verity."

BOOK 3—NOW

CONFRONTATION

Outside the Alendan Core's headquarters, Pilot X watched Alexandra approach. He wanted a confrontation. He wanted to tell her just how angry he was. How much she had cost him. How much he liked her cascading blonde hair and how that made him angrier.

"Pilot X, I'm glad I found you—"

He interrupted her sharply. "I am too. I'm glad I could help you and the Core further the ends of the war and tie it up tightly for you."

"What do you mean?" Her look of surprise was exquisitely genuine.

"Oh, that's beautiful. Maybe they didn't even tell you? I think not, though. You all knew. Your instructions not to arrive during the conflicts were perfect. I tied up each battle neatly. I thought I was preserving the rest of the universe. Turned out I was keeping the rest of time from ever finding out about the extent of the war that rages behind my shields."

"No. I suppose it might seem that way—"

"It might seem that way, I suppose," he cut her off savagely, "if the Secretary hadn't met me in the time of the final battle. Which, by the way, wasn't the final battle at all but only a convenient place to tell me my work was done. Clever. You should have told him not to spill the beans. I would have come back here anyway to find out what was wrong."

"The final battle was not a battle?"

"No, it wasn't. But every other one was. And I cleaned them up so well. One had several destroyed planets. I cleaned that one up into a rather implausible moon and an asteroid belt. You'd never know it even happened. Scientists there in later eras are probably puzzled by the moon's existence, but you know scientists. They always think of something to explain away the odd."

"The last battle should have been the apocalypse. That was where you were—" This time she was cut off by Aelreda, who had just arrived.

"What are you telling her?" Aelreda snapped.

"The truth," Pilot X snapped back.

"What truth?"

Pilot X told her what the Secretary had said. Aelreda looked crestfallen. This scared Pilot X more than anything else.

"You didn't know," he said.

Aelreda could only shake her head. Tears came to her eyes.

"They've beaten us," Aelreda finally sputtered.

"No," said Alexandra. "You can still make this right. I know you can." Her eyes bored into Pilot X, piercing his heart.

"Oh no," he yelled, backing away. "Once burned, twice turned. I am not falling for that one again. I couldn't help you, even if I was stupid enough," he scoffed. "They have Verity."

"And you've removed all your possessions?" asked Alexandra.

"What?"

"You can't store them there. It's against regulations."

"Why do you care?"

"Because it's your excuse to get back in. And your excuse to steal her."

"Steal who?"

Alexandra looked surprised. "Well, Verity."

"Oh." Pilot X thought about it. "Oh no . . . well, maybe. But not for you."

THEFT

Pilot X carried nothing as he approached the guard shack.

"Greetings, Ambassador X," the guard said. "What can I do for you?"

"Just Pilot X, Guard . . ."

"Henta. Guard Henta."

"Guard Henta. Just came to get my things out of Verity," said Pilot X nonchalantly.

"Oh." The guard looked pained. She obviously respected Pilot X and didn't want to deny him anything. "The *Verity* is on lockdown right now on strict orders from the Council. Nobody allowed in or out."

"Understandable," Pilot X said with an easy smile. "And I won't touch her controls. Just need to get my stuff out."

"I'm sorry," Guard Henta said slowly. "I'm not allowed to make exceptions."

Pilot X frowned. It was a friendly frown. The frown you have for a friend who's in a hard position. "You're not allowed to break regulations either."

"Exactly." Guard Henta relaxed.

"And one regulation says you can't allow storage of personal effects for unassigned personnel in unassigned capsules, right?"

Guard Henta unrelaxed. "Yes, that's true."

"So if you don't let me get my things, you're essentially letting me store them in the *Verity*."

"I see what you're saying, but—"

"I know." Pilot X shook his head. "It's unfair that they put people in these situations."

Guard Henta seemed frozen.

"Just between you and me, what are the actual orders restricting Verity?" Pilot X asked.

"Well. No one is allowed to enter, activate, or modify the *Verity* until further notice. No exceptions."

"Ah. I don't have any reason to activate or modify her if I just want to get my things. So I'd only be violating the entry provision. However, if I leave my things in there, then I'm violating the entire regulation."

"I guess so."

"When did the restriction on the *Verity* come down?"

"Right after I started my rotation."

"Do you constantly check orders while on duty?"

Guard Henta puffed up a bit. "I make it a point of pride to check in regularly."

Pilot X inwardly groaned at her pride in obedience. "But it's possible that orders come in that you don't see right away."

She deflated a bit. "I guess so."

"Could happen to anybody!" he reassured her. "You just let me get my stuff, I'll be gone, and you say you saw the orders after I left. Right?"

Guard Henta looked unsure. "I don't want to lie—"

"And you don't have to. Just don't volunteer that you saw the orders before I came. Honestly, if I just leave with my stuff and the *Verity* is locked up tight, no one will care."

"What if something goes wrong?"

"You blame me!" Pilot X said cheerily.

"Oh, I wouldn't want to do that." Guard Henta looked shocked.

"It's OK. I can take it. Deal?"

Guard Henta came to a decision and nodded. Pilot X motioned Alexandra to come over to his side.

"Who's that?" Guard Henta objected.

"I need help carrying things," Pilot X explained easily.

"Oh, right. OK. Make it quick."

"We will," Pilot X reassured her. They hurried toward the *Verity*. Pilot X felt bad about Guard Henta. She was so sincere.

CHOICE

Pilot X asked Verity to land in a hidden field on the far side of Alenda while he figured out what to do next. He would have jumped in time too, but Alexandra was a member of the Alendan Core and forbidden to travel in time. Besides, they would look for him to jump through time. Jumping only in space might be a better disguise anyhow.

"So what's the plan?" Alexandra asked.

Pilot X looked skeptical but said nothing.

"To what plan is she referring?" asked Verity.

Pilot X sighed. "As you know, we've been duped. Alexandra here thinks by stealing you, I can somehow undo the damage and still stop the war. But I'll be honest, I have no idea where to even start. I only went through the plan this far in order to get you back, Verity, and to have an excuse to spend more time with Alexandra."

Alexandra blushed.

"You have all you need for such a plan," said Verity.

"Lovely," scoffed Pilot X. "You've moved on from humor to poetry."

"Is that poetic?"

"Sort of," said Alexandra when Pilot X didn't answer.

"Noted," said Verity. "But I was not attempting to be poetic. I was hoping to assist the beginning of your planning."

"What do you mean?" Alexandra asked.

"Yes, what *do* you mean?" Pilot X repeated.

"You have in your possession a gift from the Progons, no?" Verity asked.

Pilot X nodded without changing his confused expression.

"And some remains from the Sensaurians. That matter you found stuck to our side."

He nodded slowly. He'd almost forgotten about that. After the Sensaurians had pelted the *Verity* with pieces of themselves, he'd scraped a piece off the hull to examine later.

"The Progon gift is a communicator; the Sensaurian remains contain telepath generators, as do all their cells. Your display generator can combine with an Inverter-Chrono-integrator, which we have stored in the singularity chamber. You can use those to create the Instant and remove the war without destroying all people or all timelines."

"What?" Alexandra and Pilot X said in unison.

"How do you know this?" Pilot X said.

"So all of us will survive?" asked Alexandra.

"I cross-referenced available information on the Instant with the items' capabilities and verified the potentiality. I am ninety-seven percent confident it would work as expected. However, not all would survive. The three civilizations of the war would be eliminated."

"What?! Why do you think I would do that?" Pilot X shouted.

"Because of all the devastation you've seen," answered Alexandra slowly. "Devastation that you now know the Alendans were just as responsible for. You can still preserve most threads. That's thousands of civilizations. You'll not only bring multiple civilizations back from the dead but also give them whole futures they never could have had in the current timeline. Only the three warring civilizations will be affected directly, right, Verity?" she asked.

"That is correct. Its use would cause a transdimensional rift that would eliminate all Alendans, Sensaurians, and Progons from history. To an observer who doesn't know better, it would appear that material of the universe is missing or undetectable. A dark sort of matter," Verity concluded.

"Think of it." Alexandra's beautiful eyes sparkled. "Yes, a universe without Alendans, but without Sensaurians and Progons too. A universe where the most devastating war possible disappears. By sealing off the war and hiding the battles, you could make this possible. You can remove the war from space-time, Pilot X."

He thought hard about it. Could he destroy his people? All his people? Not end their lives but end their entire existence. Wipe them from history. His people had done that to thousands of other civilizations. But that didn't make it right. Or did it? He could save and extend trillions of potential lives, rejuvenate thousands of whole civilizations across billions of years. It was immeasurable. But he had to sacrifice two civilizations he did not care for and one he was a member of.

"How could I do that?"

Alexandra put her hand on his.

"You can't. Not if you think of it as ending Alenda. You know how time threads work. You will be protected and exist in this new thread. This thread you're in now must still have some reality for you to make that transition. So all you're doing is stanching a wound. You've seen the complete depth and breadth of this universe. Is it not worth creating a new one so we can learn from the mistakes of this one?"

Alexandra stared deeply into his eyes. "You have the unique set of skills to give us a second chance. And by us, I mean existence. And your purpose once you've done this will be to tell the story of *this* universe to that new one. Help them not to make the same mistakes. Don't allow Sensaurians or Progons or Alendans or anything like them to rise again."

Pilot X nodded. He thought of the destroyed systems he had barely preserved. He thought of the planets that suffered under the despotism of the fifty Manic Masters. He remembered the massive battlegrounds and frozen bodies flung into space from the unrelenting bombardments. He thought of Yeoman Alphaea on Mersenne. How he wanted his children to play in the forest.

He looked down for a long time. Nobody spoke. He finally looked up again. "And you'll come with me?"

Alexandra lowered her eyes. "I can't. You know I can't travel in time."

"How does that make sense? You're not preserving the timeline anymore if the timeline disappears and you with it."

Alexandra laughed.

"Why is that funny?" Pilot X said.

"Because that's exactly why I can't go with you. These threads have to have some reality for you to carry this out. If I leave, I weaken them. Even if it's just a little, it's too much."

"Then I'll come back for you. After. Somehow."

She smiled and shook her head as the tears flowed out. "You won't. You can't. And you shouldn't. But it won't matter because you can't."

"Verity?"

"Alexandra's basis for staying in her timeline is sound."

"And?"

"Probability of being able to return to this thread after a timeline reset cannot be calculated."

"You hear that?" Pilot X said.

Alexandra nodded. "I do. I hear it more clearly than you, Pilot X. It means good-bye." And she cried. And he cried.

And they kissed good-bye.

OBSERVERS

"What is that?! A ship? How did it get in there? It's identified as the *Verity*."

"Is that Ambassador X?"

"He's not Ambassador anymore. He's gone rogue, didn't you hear?"

"Citizen X, please cease your activities and vacate at once!"

"Citizen? No need to insult the man if you want him to comply."

"What's he doing?"

"My stars, how did he get that?"

"He's not going to use it, is he?!"

"Ambassador X, stop this minute."

Foomp.

THE END AS BEGINNING

An echo rumbled through the tower as the *Verity* settled into place outside the abandoned lunar command center. The sky above burned with millions of lights, all representing destruction. The tower was on a moon orbiting Mersenne, which burned below.

Pilot X left the *Verity* and began his work on the bare rock surface of the moon. He thought about his conversation with Captain Alphaea so long ago. The Yeoman had gone on to run a planet that could now no longer be run.

Mersenne wasn't even a target, just collateral damage in this three-way war. As Pilot X worked, he thought about how he'd been tricked into hiding the war's existence.

A shimmer appeared in the distance. Pilot X stopped what he was doing for a moment and grabbed a scanner to investigate. He couldn't possibly have been followed. He zoomed in and saw a small intrasystem craft had settled neared the remains of the base. Three figures were carrying luggage out of the craft. Their clothes barely deserved the name. They were covered in grime and thin as wraiths. The tallest of the three seemed familiar. Pilot X looked closer. It was Captain Alphaea. The other two were what was left of his children. They disappeared inside the rubble of the base in a desperate attempt to flee the destruction above.

Pilot X looked at the device he had assembled in front of him and finished the last few pieces. The Instant. It was ready. The *Verity* was plugged in, providing coordinates. The Progon transmitter was humming. The Sensaurian material presumably awaiting his command.

He made himself think of the other people who would never be if he activated the Instant. Of the lives irrevocably changed. They wouldn't realize it, of course. The Instant cut time at the base, causing the timeline to repair itself like a wound. Its inhabitants would assume that things had always been the way they were. No. That wasn't right. They wouldn't even assume. The idea of things not being what they were would never occur. Pilot X wondered how many times this had happened. A useless word, *times*, given the nature of this.

Only he would remember. He and Verity sheltered within the bubble of the Instant's operating field. He alone would carry the memories of a broken universe. He alone would carry the responsibility of wiping out and replacing everyone. This made him neither god nor devil. It only made him responsible.

And he feared that. He shied from it. He desperately thought of a way around it, a way to bring the three parties to peace. But he had seen all of this war now. He knew how it ended. With nobody. No system left unscathed. No one left to carry the lesson. That was the biggest crime. The Alendans knew this would not end with a better universe, and yet they persisted.

He thought about the destruction of countless systems. He thought about the Alendan Council's arrogance and laughter at how they had manipulated him. He thought about the dead. He realized the Alendans didn't care. He thought about Captain Alphaea, cowering in the nearby rubble with his children, unaware of the danger lurking nearby in the hands of Pilot X.

Nobody made him do this. Nobody knew for sure that he was here. Nobody was depending on him. This was his choice. His hand shook.

He flipped the switch.

X

The lights disappeared in an instant. Like turning off a light switch. For a moment he thought he might have destroyed everything in the universe but himself. But a dim glow from the *Verity* showed he still had rock beneath his feet. As his eyes adjusted, he could make out stars and even the faint glow of Mersenne in the distance. The nearby base and its rubble, along with its occupants, were gone.

He cried. The unstoppable wave had raced through space and time to the fringes of the universe, destroying some, rewriting history for the rest.

It had happened so fast. He felt like he could flick the switch the other way and it would all come back. But of course it wouldn't. That's not how it worked. He flicked the switch anyway. Nothing happened.

He sobbed.

He had done it. He had irrevocably destroyed his own timeline. But he had stopped them. His people. And their enemies. A war that had unleashed a million maniacs on unsuspecting worlds. A war that killed so many innocents, leaving him no choice but to take this action, at this moment, irrevocably.

He had not just destroyed, though.

What had replaced it? Was it something better?

That was his purpose now, to explore this new timeline. To see what had changed. To do his best to make those changes positive.

The tower loomed dark behind his ship just on the edge of the protective envelope, thin and insubstantial. It would fade as soon as he left. He dragged himself into the *Verity* and told her to set course.

"Where?" she asked reasonably. Always reasonable, Verity.

He would head for the Fringe Cascade, to the limits of existence, and see how they had fared there.

Pilot X fled from the dark tower as it faded and disappeared into never having been.

APPENDIX

ENCYCLOPEDIA ALENDIA

A recovered page from an encyclopedia known only to exist in the Library of Verity.

Alendans—A race of bipedal mammals who use technology to move their whole bodies individually or in groups through time. They are a tribal culture, although largely unified in the face of contact with other species.

Alendans are born from females after genetic mixing between pairs. Alendan mothers normally give birth to one or two babies at a time, with a range of one to three babies on average in a lifetime.

Alendans are colonial and operate outposts on moons and planets in their own system and others.

Alendan society is ruled by the Guardians of Alenda, who oversee the conduct of time travel, which is central to the culture. The Guardians delegate much of their authority to a Secretary who serves as the executive of the government.

The Guardians of Alenda consider themselves the highest authority in the universe on time travel. They police the timeline and endeavor to keep time travel safe.

The Progons and Sensaurians do not recognize this authority in their own time-related activities. This has given rise to rumors of a Dimensional War between the three cultures.

Home planet: Alenda (which means "land").

Communication: Mostly vocal and written, with some hand signals.

Evolution: The Alendan species evolved from tree-based bipedal mammals, most directly from the species *Dimana alendsimia*.

Diplomacy: Representatives assigned to all cultures. Main diplomatic relationships throughout time are maintained with adversaries in different manners. In eras with diplomatic relations, a representative of Alenda is assigned to Tiel, the Progon homeworld, and a Progon automaton is assigned to Alenda.

Alendan diplomats make regular visits to the Sensaurian Mission at the Fringe Cascade but do not take up residence. The Sensaurians conduct diplomacy only in this mission.

Progons—A race of pure electricity that houses themselves in great machines.

Progons are often mistakenly thought of as a collective because of their basis in electricity. However, Progons are individuals and do not and cannot merge into a larger collective existence.

Unlike for most biological entities, the Progon evolution was not driven by replication. Progons' ancestral forms were driven by circuit completion, with replication later supporting that.

The major step for Progon civilization was inhabiting Proroqs, which allowed them mobility. Proroqs are natural forms that can move easily, a feature of Tiel's geology, like small boulders with limb-like projections that can manipulate objects. They are commonly referred to as "rock carts" by non-Progons.

Primitive Progons were limited to inhabiting Proroqs but eventually learned to construct larger and more efficient machines. As they spread out on their planet, they programmed automata to build ever more impressive and complex cities. Eventually, Progons developed automata that could leave the planet and even explore other worlds.

Actual Progon individuals exist in circuits inside the great machines on Tiel. They rarely leave or interact with outsiders. The Progons most Alendans might encounter are simply robots or other automata controlled from Tiel.

Home planet: Tiel (which means "one").

Communication: Progons can send electrical signals over distance and through time. They can explore the universe without leaving their home planet. Their automata expand and sometimes conquer other worlds while under homebound Progon control.

While Progon circuits are capable of traveling off planet, it is extremely rare for an actual Progon to leave the planet.

Evolution: Some theories suggest Progons caused their own evolution by sending instructions to primitive Progons to guide them in creating machines outside the Proroqs. The Progons deny this, saying it is impractical to communicate anything of significance to primitive Progons.

Most scientists believe the paradox could not be balanced and accept Progon assurances that it has not occurred. Alendans have visited Progon history and have not found any evidence of interference from the future in their evolution.

Diplomacy: Progon automata are warlike, and the Progons have expanded to rule over large amounts of space centered around Tiel and the other Progon central worlds.

Progons and Sensaurians have no diplomatic relations, but keep an uneasy distance between their two cultures. Alendans have fought fierce wars with the Progons at times but also maintain long stretches of peacetime. In eras of good diplomatic relations, diplomats are often placed on Tiel and Progon automata are stationed on Alenda.

Accusations of a secret Dimensional War have persisted between the three cultures, but no evidence for such a war has yet been uncovered.

Sensaurians—A unified megaorganism that can split up into smaller bits down to single cells. Sensaurians can send parts of themselves back in time. The culture is extremely isolated and little is known of their history.

Home planet: Sensaur (meaning "us").

Communication: Instant hive mind thought transfer limited only by speed of light but enhanced through anticipatory nonlocal neural transfer.

Evolution: Unknown.

Diplomacy: Sensaurian mission at Fringe Base located off the Fringe Cascade. This is the only Sensaurian location for diplomatic business.

ABOUT THE AUTHOR

Tom Merritt is an award-winning independent tech podcaster and host of regular tech news and information shows. Tom cohosts *Sword & Laser*, a science fiction and fantasy podcast, book club, and publishing imprint, with Veronica Belmont. Tom has published several science fiction and technology books, including *Citadel 32: A Tale of the Aggregate*, *The Year in Tech History*, *Sword & Laser Anthology*, and *Lot Beta*. He lives in Los Angeles with his wife and two dogs.

LIST OF PATRONS

This book was made possible in part by the following grand patrons who preordered the book on Inkshares.com. Thank you.

Adam Gomolin

Avalon Marissa Radys

Christian Fletcher

Donald Jaramillo

H. John Vogel

Jarrett Crowe

J-F. Dubeau

Justin Zellers

Kari Simms

Katherine A. Napier

Kimberly Price

Matt Kaye

Michael J. Aikins

Mike McPeek

Nathan Lawrence

Paul Dow

Philip Wenger

Ryan D. Johnson

Steven Rod

Wayne Williamson

INKSHARES

Inkshares is a crowdfunded book publisher. We democratize publishing by having readers select the books we publish—we edit, design, print, distribute, and market any book that meets a preorder threshold.

Interested in making a book idea come to life? Visit inkshares.com to find new book projects or to start your own.

SWORD & LASER

Sword & Laser is a science fiction and fantasy-themed book club, video show, and podcast that gathers together a strong online community of passionate readers to discuss and enjoy books of both genres.

Listen in or join the conversation at swordandlaser.com.